Dweepa

OXFORD NOVELLAS
Encompassing literature, popular and genre fiction, writers old and new, this series presents an orchestra of Indic voices

Series Editor: Mini Krishnan

Other titles in the Series

Vaadivaasal (Tamil)
C.S. Chellappa

Tyanantar (Marathi)
Saniya

Sheet Sahasik Hemantolok (Bengali)
Nabaneeta Dev Sen

*Jeevichirikkunnavarkku
Vendiyulla Oppees* (Malayalam)
Johny Miranda

Moogavani Pillanagrovi (Telugu)
Kesava Reddy

Dweepa
Island

Na. D'Souza

Translated from Kannada by
Susheela Punitha

OXFORD
UNIVERSITY PRESS

OXFORD
UNIVERSITY PRESS

Oxford University Press is a department of the University of Oxford.
It furthers the University's objective of excellence in research,scholarship,
and education by publishing worldwide. Oxford is a registered trademark of
Oxford University Press in the UK and in certain other countries

Published in India by
Oxford University Press
YMCA Library Building, 1 Jai Singh Road, New Delhi 110 001, India

ISBN-13: 978-0-19-809744-0
ISBN-10: 0-19-809744-1

Typeset in Berling LT Std 10/15.5,
at MAP Systems, Bengaluru 560 082, India
Printed in India at Akash Press, New Delhi 110 020

*To the hope that we will learn to
cherish the Earth which has nurtured*

CONTENTS

Series Editor's Note

*'Freedom is knowing and understanding things
quite other than ourselves.'*

–Anonymous

Writers have always experimented with forms in their search
for the best vehicles for their thoughts, moods, and words.
While there might be arguments about what length defines
the genre, the novella was shaped and recognized in the late
nineteenth century as allowing for greater development
of theme and character than a short story without being
burdened with the demands of a full-length novel.

Our broad goal in assembling the Oxford Novellas,
a unique series combining substance and brevity, is to
present the least studied genre from one of the world's
oldest literary traditions which includes one of the
most sophisticated pre-modern poetic theories. At a

time when news is entertainment and literature has to compete with popular fiction, two criteria have guided our selections: socially relevant themes for readers who might want to know things quite outside their experience and understanding, and literary excellence. Thus, famous names march with writers few people have even heard of.

Having absorbed words from nearly four hundred languages, English is opulently equipped to interpret and express the cultural energy of the regions it once entered as the colonizer's voice. If, to paraphrase Wittgenstein, the limits of our language mark the limits of our world, we hope, from time to time, through this series, to move the borders of literary enjoyment further and ever further. Translation into English brings together the creative potential of different Indian languages, the special understanding of the world each one of those languages has, and consequently, the distinctive way they carry the memories and histories of those who use them.

The art of story-telling and the art of narration mingle to give us a literary mosaic made possible by translators working to move texts originally written in other languages into English. We believe that the translator is not merely an echo or a shadow, a reflection or a crib, but a fresh, strong supporting voice that conveys both the said and the equally vital 'unsaid' parts of the original into the receiving language.

MINI KRISHNAN

Author's Note

The problem of submersion of land in the cause of modernization and the ensuing displacement of the local people is something that has bothered me for a long time.

I worked for about twenty-five years in areas connected with the Sharavathi hydroelectric project. In 1959, when Shri S.K. Patil, Minister for Power at the Centre, pressed a button and inaugurated the project, a huge boulder split into a thousand pieces and stones rained on the tin shed where we were taking shelter. Over the next five years, the Linganamakki Dam came into existence. Slowly, the Sharavathi River deepened not regarding the forests, valleys, canals, villages, the villagers and their agricultural lands.

The villagers were compensated with money and land elsewhere. I have seen people dismantling their homes, loading their extended families and their belongings onto lorries and bullock carts, and going away to wherever land was allotted to them. But who helped them cope with their grief and fear, having to uprooted themselves from everything familiar, from a way of life based on a value system they had known for generations? Nobody thought of that. On the other hand, crafty government officials exploited these people who were ignorant of the ways of the outside world. They sought bribes, they harassed and cheated them.

I poured my sorrow at their plight into *Dweepa* (Island). It is the story of a man who is forced to lose his community identity and fails to cope with his new-found individuality. I also wrote three other novels based on different aspects of the theme of displacement: *Mulugade* (Submersion) which won a prize in the Ugadi issue of *Sudha*, a weekly, in 1983; *Oddu* (Dam/ Barricade); and *Gunavanthe* (A Worthy Woman).

Dweepa came out in 1970 in *Prakasha*, a weekly from Manipal. The late K.V. Subbanna, founder of the world famous institute for drama, Ninasam, was interested in making it into a film. However, in 1978, he said, 'I am not sure if I will be able to make it into a movie but I will publish it through Akshara Prakashana.'

That is how it was published in his press for the first time. Later I was happy to hear that Subbanna had given the story to his nephew, Girish Kasaravalli, to explore its potential for a movie. The film version of *Dweepa* won the President's Gold Medal in 2006 besides many other awards. The novella was published again in 2004 by Ravindra Prakashana together with an article by Girish Kasaravalli and a few stills from the movie.

I am happy that *Dweepa* has now been translated into English. The tragedy in the lives of these innocent victims of modernization will now merge with the groans of the oppressed the world over, wherever this story is read. It is a fitting way to perpetuate the memory of those who lose all they hold dear wherever the country develops at their cost. It is also a proper way of mourning what we have lost because of what we have gained.

My thanks are due to the late K.V. Subbanna and Ravindra Prakashana who have made this story available in print, Girish Kasaravalli and his team who made the award-winning movie, and Mini Krishnan, my editor. Mini is not only a committed editor of repute but also a visionary. In showcasing the plight of the less fortunate in our society through translations of regional literature, she is striving to bring about a social change for the better that includes them. I wish her efforts every success. I thank Susheela Punitha for translating *Dweepa* into English and for the profound discussions we have had about the text over the phone.

NA. D'SOUZA

Translator's Note

I learnt about the need for elaboration in translation while translating *Dweepa*, a novella with eloquent silences, the silence of the voiceless and the silence of the stifled. The silences spill over to the reader to stay on after the reading is done. What can one *say* about bonded labourers being bundled out like commodity to be rearranged wherever their masters may resettle? Or about displaced village communities being socially regressed in the name of progress and development? Silence alone can provide the space for introspection and grief.

But to a translator, reading is not a passive skill. She is actively looking for ways to transfer the impact of the original into English, to translate the meanings embedded in the silences that follow cryptic expressions. And she learns the principle behind elaboration first-hand. For instance, take the case of the bonded labourers, Hasalara Byra and Hala. In Kannada, one word is sufficient to describe the anguish of their social condition: *huttaalugalu*. A pause after the word is, perhaps, all that a reader needs to make the necessary cultural and social connections with their plight. But translating it into English literally as *labourers from birth* would puzzle a reader unaware of a social system in India that could withhold the basic right to freedom from a person and his progeny in the guise of helping him out in an emergency. A pause would follow the expression, no doubt, but it would be vacuous with perplexity, not pregnant with grief. The connotative value of the expression required an extended explanation in English: *They were bonded labourers; bonded from birth to their masters as repayment of debt owed by their father.* I was uncomfortable with the verbosity until I realized the elaboration was necessary to fill the silence that follows it with meaning. And in English the pause can stretch to make time for the significance of the social condition to sink it in. Further elaborations in the translation blended seamlessly with the original text, until the story reached its final crescendo in a stifled scream.

Once I came to grips with the theory of elaboration through a hands-on experience with the process, I was happy to use it in place of cumbersome footnotes to ease the flow of the narrative. And I knew my editor, Mini Krishnan, would be happy too, for it was she who had suggested that I should work the meaning of expressions into the context to keep the footnotes to a minimum. I am grateful to her for her meticulous care in reading the text and pointing out turgid phrases that had to be reworked. I am lucky that she cannot read Kannada and does not take certain meanings in the text for granted as I do as an insider! She has helped to make the story in English more lucid. My thanks are also due to Na. D'Souza for reading every chapter as I sent it to him, checking it for the transference of flavour and of details of the historical situation he has presented in the story.

I thank Rajendra Chenni and V.S. Sreedhara for their invaluable review of the text. I thank Chenni especially for his insightful comment that the descriptions are the story. This translation would not have been possible without our collaborative effort.

My special thanks to my family. My husband, children, and grandchildren have been a tremendous support in this venture.

SUSHEELA PUNITHA

Introduction

Dweepa is one of the few novels in Kannada that has development-induced destruction as its central theme. In fact, its author, Na. D'Souza is known in Kannada literary circles as a 'submersion writer', a reference to the many stories he has written about people and families affected by big dams. It is equally important to note that he wrote about the travails of displacement created by the construction of big dams much before 'development' became a matter of prime concern, and a focus of critical attention by social activists, policymakers, and writers. Of course, it has become a universal mantra of progress in contemporary Indian politics and is used as a cover-up to usher in neo-liberal policies, structural adjustment programmes, and even communal violence. At the same time, it has led to various social movements and protests with issues ranging from environmental protection and livelihood questions to upholding human rights.

However, none of these issues occupied centre stage, as they do now, when *Dweepa* was first published in 1970 in the special issue of a weekly. (It appeared as a book in 1978.) It was a time when the growth model had not reached today's menacing proportions and India still looked forward to more developmental work. Though there was widespread disillusionment with the Nehruvian model of progress, the criticism was mainly against the dynastic rule and the monopoly of Congress. The growing sycophancy in the Congress and a marked deviation from the promised path of socialism were considered the main threats to democracy. It was a time when to be a modernist writer meant a refusal to accept traditional values and to look for authentic experience. It is interesting to note that the advent of literary modernity in Kannada coincided with this disillusionment with Nehruvian policy. Poet Gopalkrishna Adiga, who is seen as a harbinger of Kannada modernism, even wrote a poem titled 'Nehru Never Retires' which critiqued the hypocrisy of the so-called high culture. The anti-Nehru sentiment also permeated the thought and writings of the three major modernist writers of that time, U.R. Ananthamurthy,

P. Lankesh, and Poornachandra Tejaswi, in spite of their different approaches to modernity. All of them were equally influenced by Mahatma Gandhi and Ram Manohar Lohia, and shared a common disbelief in Marxist thought. However, their critique of the Nehru era was directed not so much against his model of progress as against the misrule and an abandonment of socialist concerns. The growing schism between promise and performance in the polity found its literary expression in the form of a search for an authentic self coloured by a sense of disquiet, together leading to an exploration of new values. Thus literary modernism in Kannada was constituted by an angst borne by a struggle to cope with life in all its complexity.

Overall, it can be said that Kannada literary modernity was characterized, among other things, by its portrayal of a fragmented self, caused mainly due to fractured democracy resulting in a sense of alienation. Its major concern was to develop a critique of a fossilized culture that was insensitive to the plight of the common people. However, it is important to note that these writers, at that point of time, did not see fragmentation as a handiwork of the new model of development, based on greed and unlimited exploitation of natural resources. It is only later, particularly after the 1990s, that we see Kannada writers, especially Ananthamurthy and Tejaswi, develop a critique of the ideology behind the new model of progress and development in their writings. While the former turned to an exploration of the pre-modern self, the latter took to environmental forces as a means to explore the unknown modes of being. Tejaswi's writings repeatedly point to the perils of environmental degradation and the loss to human life caused by our unlimited plunder of Earth's resources. This shift is understandable as it reflects a growing pan-Indian concern for protecting nature from human greed, thanks to the advent of several important and influential gender- and environment-based social movements which gathered momentum during the late 1980s. These movements opened new ways of conceptualizing the world and unleashed new ideas related to the question of 'being in the world' with a force that no writer could ignore.

Meanwhile, literary modernity in Kannada had undergone a shift. By the 1970s, it had lost its force, thanks to the rise of various protest movements like Bandaya and Dalit, resulting in the awakening of a new social consciousness that questioned the excessive preoccupation with the insulated individual self of the modernist era. The evidence of an awakening of Shudra consciousness in literature was already evident in writers like Kuvempu, but it was framed within a broad liberal humanistic outlook. The new Dalit-Bandaya movement, however, was different in the sense that it drew the active participation of writers from the marginalized communities and was even supported by early modernist writers like Lankesh and Tejaswi. The extreme subjectivity that had invaded Kannada modernity came under attack. This resulted in an altered sensibility and a demand for new aesthetics, and writers turned away from an excessive obsession with the individual predicament and showed a much more active engagement with societal issues. In other words, it was a great turning point in Kannada writing as it moved from an acute sense of the 'private' to a more nuanced 'public' domain.

D'Souza did not identify himself with any of these literary movements, though his writing career began in the mid-1960s and continued during the subsequent decades. But it would be wrong to say that he was a complete outsider and was untouched by their influence. He wrote at a time when Navya and later Bandaya movements were at their peak, but he did not declare his affiliation to any particular movement like many of his contemporaries did. That he was not at the forefront of any of these movements does not mean he was oblivious to their presence. At the same time, it needs to be noted that his writings do not overtly exhibit any sustained engagement with the main currents of Kannada literary movements. It is perhaps for this reason that Kannada mainstream criticism, obsessed as it is with a sense of aesthetic excellence and a tendency to view anything 'popular' with scepticism, has not paid serious attention to his writings. And D'Souza is not alone in this treatment, a point that has also been noted by some critics.

Given his active interest and participation, even to this day, in various social movements, particularly related to environmental issues, in and around Sagar town where he lives, it would be unfair to describe him as a mute spectator confined to the margins. Perhaps he felt there was no need to be a part of any particular literary movement to write what he felt passionately about. His strength as a writer seems to stem from his ability to remain open to the ideas generated by movements as well as maintain a critical distance from them. This is not to suggest, as some critics are fond of suggesting, that as a writer he stands 'above all ideologies'. On the contrary, it may well be the case that he can observe life from close quarters without being swayed by any one particular dominating point of view. This quality, coupled with his simple narrative style, will perhaps explain his popularity as a writer. His wide range of creative output – he is one of the most prolific writers in Kannada with nearly a hundred works to his credit – stands testimony to the fact that he has a larger number of readers than many of his contemporaries.

Having worked in the Sharavathi River Valley project, he had witnessed the entire activity of dam building from beginning to end, and had observed the apathy of bureaucracy. He had first-hand experience of studying the project's effects on the lives of poor and marginalized village folk. Moreover, he had moved closely among people living in interior forests, not as a part of his work, but as his own calling.

Viewed in this context, it is not surprising that many of his novels and short stories deal with the issue of submergence leading to displacement and provide an insider's view of the great sustaining force that enables the poor to face both natural and man-made adversities with great dignity and poise despite tragic consequences. Apart from several short stories, three of his novels, *Dweepa* (Island, 1978), *Mulugade* (Submersion, 1984), and *Oddu* (Dam/Barricade, 1990), deal with the tragedy of families being displaced due to highly insensitive and destructive 'development' projects. Each of them throws light on different aspects of this modern tragedy. While *Dweepa* portrays the agony caused by the rising backwater, leading to separation of human lives and hearts, *Oddu* depicts the heartlessness of bureaucracy which refuses to provide compensation for families whose lands are above the full reservoir level, but nevertheless marooned by the backwater. Absurd as it may sound, these are real stories and there are people still fighting for justice in many parts of Karnataka. It is the uncertainty of survival that finally leads to the tragic end. *Mulugade*, on the other hand, provides a picture of how people negotiate their destinies differently once they leave their ancestral homes and start their lives afresh. While very few manage to make their lives better, others do not and some even find in it an opportunity to exploit the situation at the cost of hapless victims of displacement. The three novels can be read as a trilogy, and together they offer a kaleidoscopic depiction of the complexities of human life, the avoidable loss of certain forms of living and belief systems, and the inevitability of negotiating new modes of being. The turbulence within the serene-looking, placid backwater is barely visible, but D'Souza dives deep and brings into view the tragedy of separated hearts, their unfulfilled dreams, and the loss of a way of life itself.

Dweepa brings a close-up view of life in a remote hamlet facing submergence and provides an insider's view of what it means to live amidst the fear of being marooned. Rendered in his usual style of simple and straight narration, the novella unfolds the tragedy that awaits the only family left behind, struggling to put its life together in a remote area that is soon going to be an island. Though there are several novels in Kannada with nature functioning as a living presence in the backdrop, in very few of them does nature become a character, driving the plot of the novel to its final destiny. *Dweepa* is one such work where the river Sharavathi, now bound by a dam, frames the narrative and remains in the foreground till the novel reaches its denouement. It reflects the changing mood of the protagonists, sometimes threatening and at other times protective. The river's eternal companion, rain, also plays a significant role. The chapters are named after the stars that influence the different phases of the monsoon, each suggesting a different mood and behaviour of the rains corresponding to the changes that happen in quick succession in the lives of the three individuals that inhabit the novella. Thus, nature, both as an external presence and an internal force, shapes the structure of the novella, pushing it to its final resolution.

At the very beginning we are told that the three families that came to inhabit the small patch of land at the foot of Sita Parvatha, a small hillock, had to struggle against nature to establish their settlements. There is a suggestion that this is a sort of benevolent intervention that nature tolerates and even nurtures the labouring human beings to enjoy the fruits of their work. Their status depended not so much on how much land they owned but on the fact that they did have some cultivable land. In fact, the novella opens with this remark:

Ganapayya was neither rich nor poor. All he had were two acres of wetland for arecanut and three acres of agricultural land to grow rice. He did not own any farm hands; he hired some for wages. But that did not make any difference to his status. The respect the landlords commanded came from their place and role in the community, not from their wealth. This had been the system in the Malenadu villages for generations.

Ganapayya's family may not be as rich or as comfortably placed as the other two, but there is a suggestion that they lived as equals and even depended on one another, despite the difference in their economic status. But once Ganapayya learns that he is not going to receive the compensation as easily as others had received theirs, doubts begin to crop up. Ganapayya not only feels left out, but also feels he has been discriminated against. This makes him feel inferior to others and fills him with rage and even self-doubt. This is the first sign of the dam causing an unspoken rift, a small hiatus in the natural bonding that existed earlier. This sense of inferiority affects his relations with his wife, Nagaveni, and reaches a crescendo after the arrival of Krishnayya. There is a suggestion in the novella that the fissures that develop in the couple's relationship may not entirely be of their own making. There is an external force in the form of the dam that slowly inundates the village as well as the complex web of relationships that had sustained them at other adverse times.

> 'I can't eat a wholesome meal. I can't sleep to forget my troubles. I can't speak with my heart open. I can't trust anyone as my own, hug anyone as mine,' thought Krishnayya, 'the householder, Ganapayya might be feeling the same way. Nagaveni too. Each of us is shackled to a log but we can't sit still; we have to carry it on our heads and carry on with whatever needs to be done. Added to that, I feel there's a thorn in my heel festering, hurting at every step…. Ayyo, What a life!'

The dam becomes a symbol of man-made evil that threatens not just livelihoods but also human relations. The obstruction to the river is violence committed on Nature and hence is bound to result in counter-violence. While it submerges long-held belief-systems and values, it also brings to the fore the hidden evil, lurking in the form of a tiger that starts invading human habitation since its habitat too is disturbed. Nature, otherwise benevolent, can also reciprocate with fury when disturbed by damming. The symbolic significance of the rising water, engulfing the mythical hillock, is too hard to miss. The overbearing physical reality that surrounds and threatens their lives thus functions as a trope suggestive of their inner turmoil. *Dweepa* is as much a state of mind as it is of the outside nature.

There is also a hint in the novella that all is not over and there is a way out, if only the characters seek to know it. There is nothing inevitable about their predicament. Even though the novella moves towards a predictable ending, the tragedy that strikes them becomes poignant because it is avoidable. Look at how Krishnayya views his own condition:

> Krishnayya would have gone home if only the water around Hosamane had subsided, if only there were no wild animals on the prowl around the house. He stayed on mainly for Nagaveni's sake, for whatever pleasure she got out of his presence.

Since the time *Dweepa* was first published, displacements caused by developmental projects have taken a new turn and have risen to alarming proportions. In fact, the term 'displacement' holds the key to understanding the essential crisis of our times. It is often said that while modern India basks in the glory of its development, Bharat pays for this progress in the form of starving and struggling people. As a fictional work *Dweepa* may not capture all the complexities of development-induced disasters and the growing gap between India and Bharat that we are facing today. The simplicity of narration and the lack of density of detail that gives life force to a work of art may have prevented the novella from realizing its fiction potential. But ironically, what the novella lacks is provided by the growing complexity of our times that fills it with new meaning.

Dweepa certainly holds the unseen and untold Bharat in its womb.

V.S. SREEDHARA

Kinship Terms

amma	mother
appayya	father (appa = father, ayya = a term/suffix denoting respect)
athige	sister-in-law
ayya	familiar term of address between equals, also maharaya/maaraaya
bava/bavayya	brother-in-law
koosu	child; koose – form of addressing a child
maga	son
maani	boy
mava	father-in-law
odeya	master
sose	daughter-in-law

thatha	grandfather; familiar way of addressing an elderly person
yajamanaru	master

Krithika

Ganapayya was neither rich nor poor. All he had were two acres of wetland for an areca farm and three acres of agricultural land to grow rice. He did not own farm hands; he hired some for wages. But that did not make any difference to his status. The respect the landlords commanded came from their place and role in the community, not from their wealth. This had been the system in the Malenadu villages for generations.

When Ganapayya crossed the bridge from the farm, came down the valley, and turned towards his house, he saw the Sharavathi. An ominous bit of news about the river had been ringing in his ears. An elderly peon who had come from the Submersion Office in Kargal to see Herambha Hegde had met him with,

'Sharavathi might swallow the Hosamane Parvatha this monsoon'.

But the same man had prophesied the same doom the previous year. The Linganamakki Dam had not even risen ten feet then. The surveyors had said that the dam would not fill up. And yet, Ganapayya, Herambha Hegde, and Parameshwarayya were worried. They had hastened to the Submersion Office to check if there was any truth in what the peon had said.

'Nothing of that sort will happen,' the government officials had snapped. 'You can stay on peacefully until we compensate you with land elsewhere.'

And so they had lived without anxiety for another year. The water in the Sharavathi did not rise; the Hosamane village was not submerged. As usual, they had grown arecanut on the farms and rice in the paddy fields. And had reaped a good harvest, sold their produce, and had lived happily.

But now the dam had grown like a huge wall. They were told that water would surely collect in it this year. Would it submerge Hosamanehalli as the old man predicted?

'If that should happen, what will happen to my house?' Ganapayya feared.

Ganapayya stopped in the valley, staring at the river. The Sharavathi was just about a shout away from the row of houses. During summer she hardly held any water. But during the monsoon she was on the verge of overflowing. Even then, the water that overran the banks barely touched the paddy fields. That was about all. There was no danger to the fields or the farms. Now that the dam was being built across the river, the water level could surely rise higher. The government officials had installed a red stone on the forehead of Sita Parvatha behind the village to show how high the water would rise once the dam was ready. But the old man had insisted that the village would be inundated that very year.

'Why this year? Let it drown right now,' groaned Ganapayya in despair. 'The government has set out to ruin thousands of homes. Is it a big deal for it to drown my village, my home? But what about the compensation they say they'll give us? When will *that* come?

'All kinds of filthy strangers have stomped on our lands, measuring the fields, the farms, the house, the byre, the outhouse, the garden. They've set a price on everything. They've asked, "Where would you like us to give you land?" But that was over a year ago. Since then, there's been a monsoon, a winter, and a summer. And now the rain clouds are thundering for another monsoon. Of the five houses in the village, two belong to bonded labourers. They get no compensation, anyway, for they have nothing to call their own. The remaining three families will be duly compensated, they said.

'That Parameshwarayya may have gone to the office and greased their palms; he got his compensation pretty quickly. They've given him lands near Sagara. Herambha too might have done something of that sort. There's news that he'll be compensated very soon. But what about me? That surveyor Shetty at the Submersion Office says my file is missing, lost. I've been there over ten times now. And every time it's the same old story. And as if that's not bad enough, this old man is scaring me now. I must go again tomorrow.'

Ganapayya walked towards his house.

To one side of the village Hosamanehalli flowed the Sharavathi, on the other was Sita Parvatha. It was named after Sree Rama's wife but it was no mountain despite its name. It was neither that tall nor that wide; it was a mere hillock. Its back was lush with forestlands but its head was bald. Sree Rama, Sita, and Lakshmana were said to have come there when they were banished from Ayodhya. They had crossed the Sharavathi and had rested for a few days in a cave formed by some huge boulders near the crest of the hill. Right inside the grotto was a granite slab shaped like a cot by wind and rain. This was known as Sita-Rama's bed.

Sprawled at the foot of the hill were five families, three areca plantations, and three rice fields. Of the five families, three were those of the landlords who owned the areca farms and the paddy fields, the other two were of the bonded labourers, bonded since birth because their fathers had not been able to pay off their debts to the landlords. Of the three landlords, Herambha Hegde and Parameshwarayya were wealthy; they owned the bonded labourers of the Hasalaru community, Byra and Hala, who worked on their land.

Beyond the Sharavathi, towards the east, were towns like Talaguppa, Hiremane, and Sagara. To the west were places like Aralagodu and Bheemeshwara. The people of Hosamanehalli had contact only with the towns in the east because it was easy to cross the river during summer. The river bed was wide and strewn with huge boulders. Jumping from one to another to another, they could get to the other bank. But they could never do that during the monsoon when the Sharavathi was brimming and gushing, when not a boulder could be seen, when the water was thick and murky. No one needed to cross the river during the monsoon anyway. Even as the rainy season neared, a stock of groceries and other such commodities came from Talaguppa-Sagara, enough to last for four months. If there was still any need to go to Sagara, there was always the Thumri-Byakodi road.

These people had lived in this way for over fifty years. The coconut and jackfruit trees in front of Herambha Hegde's house spoke of the antiquity of Hosamanehalli. His house was the oldest in the village. When Herambha's grandfather left a place near Mavinagundi and bought a piece of land, built a house, and settled down here, his place came to be called Hosamane, the new house. Herambha's house became old but the village retained the name – Hosamanehalli – the village of the new house.

Now the time had come for the village to drown. Sharavathi had never come close to Hosamanehalli though she would roar ferociously from a distance during the monsoon. But she was now thinking of swallowing it up. These days her water did not flow freely; it stagnated in deep pools, waiting dangerously.

This was what Ganapayya noticed as he walked towards the house from the farm. If the flooded river gushed away in a torrent, there was always the relief of surviving a great peril. But what would happen if the flood was stalled? Or what would happen if the deluge flowed continuously? The warnings of the old man from the Submersion Office echoed in Ganapayya's ears.

The Sharavathi lay only to one side of Hosamanehalli, no doubt. But with the Linganamakki Dam coming up, it was quite possible she would overflow from all sides.

Then she could branch out on either side of the Sita Parvatha and reunite to flow on. Not just that. As the water-level rose, it would not be impossible for her to gulp down the hillock she encircled bit by bit until she swallowed it completely, once and for all. If Sita Parvatha could drown, what chance of survival did Hosamanehalli or Ganapayya-Herambha-Parameshwarayya's houses-fields-farms have? If the houses of the landlords could get submerged, what would be the plight of the labourers' hutments?

That was the reason the government had announced compensation for the displaced families; a payment at a fixed rate for farm hand, agricultural land, house, well, cowshed.... Some were also given land elsewhere. The government had provided transport to the families to move their bags and baggage to the new places. It had also sent notices to the landlords, asking them to move out before a specified date. Parameshwarayya was so unnerved on receiving the notice that he left the village almost immediately. With him went his bonded labourer, Hala, and his family.

Now there were only three houses left in Hosamanehalli: Herambha's, his farm hand Byra's, and Ganapayya's. There was a rumour that compensation had been sanctioned for Herambha. He had planted rice seedlings, hoping to stay on. But if he did get his money and was asked to move, he would have to move. And if Herambha went, Byra, his bonded labourer, would go with him. And then there would be only one house in the village – Ganapayya's!

Ganapayya strode towards his house as if he was entering a forest where a tiger lurked. Duggajja lay on a bed on a platform to one side of the veranda. He coughed and groaned on seeing his son.

'Ganapa, did Herambha meet you?'

'No, I'm coming from the farm. Why, Appayya? Did he come here?'

'Yes. He said he wanted to see you.... It looks as if he's planning to leave this year.'

'Really?'

Ganapayya had come home gripped with the fear of a lurking tiger.... Where was it hiding? In the shade of which tree? Behind which boulder? He had come home fearing from where would it spring on him and now it had sprung on him from behind. He slipped his feet back into the slippers he had just taken off and walked out again. His wife, who had been standing by the door, went indoors.

Herambha had told him they should spend the year together. He had asked for land near Ananthapura. But he had decided to stay on through the monsoon and move to the new place after the rainy season. So what had happened now for him to want to move all of a sudden? Ganapayya wiped the sweat off his face with the towel on his shoulder and walked down the valley towards Herambha's farm.

There was great commotion at the farm. People were pulling down the thatched roofing of the farmhouse. The house too was in a bustle. The cowshed was being dismantled; long wooden roofing beams were pulled down and stacked. Labourers from the Deevru community from Aralagodu were busy on the job. So it was certain that Herambha was leaving.

But why?

Seeing Ganapayya climbing up the steps to the garden, Herambha came forward.

'Ganapayya, I had been to your house. Did your father tell you?'

'Yes, he did. I just returned from the farm. I came as soon as I heard you'd come to see me. But why all this?'

'This is the reason I came to you, to tell you about this. Come here, let's sit down.'

As Ganapayya followed Herambha on to the veranda and sat on a mat with him, Herambha looked towards the door and said to his daughter, 'Koose, Ganapayya's come', but loud enough for his wife to hear him.

'My records have been finalized at the Submersion Office, Ganapayya,' he said, 'I myself saw the papers.

The farm, field, and house are valued at fifty thousand rupees for now and the money has been sanctioned. The Ananthapura land too is in my name. They have also provided money for me to clear forestland for cultivation ... I'll have to move from here today or tomorrow, anyway. Why should I stay on and strain myself through the monsoon, craving to reap a profit from harvesting areca nut and paddy? Who knows how high the water will rise this year? The hillock may not drown. But where's the guarantee that our lands won't? That's why I've decided to move. The government lorries are coming tomorrow to transport everything.'

Herambha's daughter brought a tumbler of coffee and placed it near him.

'Have this,' said Herambha.

Ganapayya lifted it to his lips mechanically. He did not know what to say about Herambha's decision. He clenched his teeth as if he had been flogged.

'Herambha ... your job's done. Where will I go? What'll I do? I've decided not to move from here until I get the compensation and land due to me. It doesn't matter if the water rises and the village drowns and all of us die ... I'll *never* move.'

'Go to the office once again, Ganapayya. They'll speed up work on your file if you bribe them some five or ten rupees.'

'I've given them, Herambha. I've given more than a hundred. All that's left is my life.'

Ganapayya took the towel off his shoulder, whacked it in disgust, and threw it on his shoulder again.

'I'll go, Herambha,' he said as he stood up and walked away briskly.

'This is just as I had feared. Once Herambha and Byra leave the place there would be just the three of us, Appayya, Nagaveni, and I. As the Sharavathi keeps rising encroaching the land around the village, the three of us will have to survive on this island for four months. We'll have no contact whatsoever with the world outside until the monsoon is over. How can we live here in this condition? I may say, enough of this problem, let's go elsewhere. But where can we go? I've depended on this farm and the field till now, where else can I live?'

'Maani, what did Herambha say?' his father asked anxiously as Ganapayya reached home.

'He's leaving, Appayya. The government has given him lands. It has sanctioned money too. He says he'll go to the new land and start cultivating it.... They were dismantling the byre.... Anyway, it's certain that he'll move with his family tomorrow or the day after.'

'Really?'

Duggajja sat staring at the areca palms swaying gently in the breeze.

'Maani, will the water come all over here this monsoon?'

'Whatever may happen, we're not moving out of here, Appayya. That's for sure.'

The old man sighed to see his son kicking the floor as he went inside the house.

And yet, this was what Duggajja had hoped for deep inside; that they would stay on at least for this year. Every time there was talk of having to leave Hosamanehalli, he felt weak in the legs and sank to the floor. He loved his piece of land with the attachment a woman feels for her mother's house. He was determined he would not leave her if he could help it. He had wondered a hundred times whether there was any way of carrying on here even when the village was covered with water. He had wished a thousand times that the dam would collapse. He had stopped every official who came on behalf of the government and had asked, 'Will Sita Parvatha really drown?' Most of them said whatever they felt the old man would like to hear from them. But some of them told him the truth; that water would stand at ten feet above the hillock. They also told him the dam would have to be built before it could hold that much of water. Some others had said there was no immediate danger to Hosamanehalli; it would take three years to complete the project.

'Why can't we stay on until then?' was Duggajja's stand, 'Where's the hurry to apply for compensation and ask for land elsewhere right now? Let it come in its own time. Anyway, we have enough to eat, don't we? Yes, water may cover the village. And yes, we may not get labourers to help on the land. But with the first rain, if we see to the planting and other such work on the farm and the field, we'll have to worry about harvesting only after the monsoon. We can always get someone to see to the odd jobs between planting and harvesting.'

That was how the old man felt but would his son feel the same way?

Ganapayya cursed the Submersion Office. He ranted as if he would go the very next day and pull down the place.

'Let's not live here during the monsoon. Let's go to my father's house,' suggested Nagaveni.

'And then? Are we to return after four months to eat cow-dung?' he roared at her, rolling up his sleeves. 'Even if the government compensates me with land and money right now, I'm not the kind who'll up and go immediately. I'm going to stay here this monsoon and reap a harvest on my land. Let whatever happens, happen.'

Ganapayya was happy when his father came inside and supported his decision.

'If you're so tired of staying here, go to your father's house,' he growled at his wife.

Another trend of thought soothed his tortured spirit: 'Anyway, Herambha's leaving his lands. Why can't I harvest them with mine? He can't uproot his rice seedlings and areca palms; he can't take them with him. And he has no one here to watch over them. Let me ask him before he leaves. He's sure to say yes. I'll tell him I'll give him a part of the harvest as his share. This seems to be a good plan. If the officials do come and bother me to leave, I can always bribe them a bit. Let's see.'

'Is the water hot for my bath, Naagu?' he asked his wife. There was spirit in his voice.

'Hmm,' replied Nagaveni. Her face was grumpy, like a shrivelled brinjal.

Ganapayya went up the attic, pulled down a pani-panche hanging from the cross pole, and wrapped the short strip of cloth around his waist. Then he loosened the full-length panche he was wearing and adjusted the *maunji* round his waist over the strip to hold it in place. Scratching his arm, he went into the bathroom.

The water came in a drainpipe cut out from areca trunks, all the way from a spring on the brow of Sita Parvatha, into his bathroom. Ganapayya's ears were attuned to the soothing sound as the water fell into a tank, *dhapa-dhapa*. Nagaveni filled a cauldron with the water, stuck a log in the fireplace, and lit it. As she left a bowl of soap nut powder for his bath and went inside, Ganapayya poured hot water on himself and sighed in great relief, 'Haa!'

The water washed away all the stress he had endured until that moment.

***

Herambha Hegde was a peculiar man; he was not at all avaricious. Though he had previously planned to stay on throughout the rainy season and harvest his produce for the year, he was willing to leave everything and move on once the compensation was sanctioned. He felt there was no need to stick on to his old way of life. He liked the new place allotted to him near Ananthapura. He was attracted to the city and so he decided to loosen the bonds that bound him to Hosamanehalli. Who knew what tomorrow would bring? He had a houseful of children, his wife was pregnant again. What if he needed help when the Sharavathi surrounded the village? What if they were marooned? What if the engineers had miscalculated and the village drowned that very monsoon? They had stayed there long enough. It was time to move on....

Herambha was ready to leave. The government lorries were packed with all his belongings, even the wooden beams, tiles, hay for thatched roof, everything.

'Herambha ...,' said Ganapayya.

'Aa, Ganapayya, I myself wanted to talk to you about that,' replied Herambha. 'Since you're going to stay on, you can harvest my fields and farm. After all, it's not as if they're *mine*. I just happened to own them, that's all. You don't have to give me a single areca nut. I've planted the rice saplings, yes. Whether you feel like giving me a share or not, it is up to you. You know why I say this? Because you'll have to work a lot more on the paddy field than I did before you can harvest it.'

And after a pause, Herambha said, 'Ganapayya, now there're only the three of you. Your father can hardly work. How much can you and your wife do? Get some farm hands from the Deevru community.'

Ganapayya nodded, 'What you say makes sense, Herambha. I'll need one or two of them for moral support besides help on the farm. Let me see if I can get some from Aralagodu or Hiremane.'

Herambha, his wife and children, Byra, his wife and children, finally bid farewell to Hosamanehalli and left. The two lorries that had been shunting back and forth for the past three days, wended their way towards the Talaguppa highway for the last time through the make-shift road beside the Sharavathi.

Ganapayya, Duggajja, and Nagamani felt depressed to see the lorries receding. They were filled with a vague dread too as if the isolation was ominous. They felt a sudden urge to up and go. But these feelings were temporary. Ganapayya slung his axe over his shoulder and set out to chop firewood to be stocked for the monsoon. As Belli ambled towards the cowshed, Nagaveni ran in to prevent the cow from feeding all her milk to her calf. The old man kept watch over the *happala* drying in the sun lest crows should get at them. The air that came to them over the Sharavathi was cool and comforting. So were the wispy white clouds.

***

Ganapayya went to the Submersion Office in Kargal.

'Oho, how is it that you've come this far, Swami?' said the old peon sitting at the door of the officer's chamber, displaying all his rotten teeth. Ganapayya pushed him aside and barged into the room.

'Both Parameshwarayya and Herambha Hegde have received compensation for their property in Hosamanehalli. What sin have I committed that I shouldn't get mine, Swami?' he asked the officer, 'Do you wish that my father, my wife, and I should meet our death by water this monsoon?'

The officer was a mild-mannered person, a very patient man. He understood the brusque ways of villagers like Ganapayya.

'Please sit down,' he said. Ganapayya sat on a stool. He felt he should not have shouted so rudely. And so he started all over again and presented his petition courteously. The officer pressed the bell on his table and asked the peon to call the person concerned.

The surveyor who had been to Hosamanehalli came in and stood in front of him trembling with fear.

'What is this, Shetty? This person says his case has not been settled yet. Why?'

'It's settled, Saar. The cheque is ready.' Shetty looked shifty, uncomfortable.

'What do you mean by "it's settled"? Have you given land and other compensations to all the families in Hosamanehalli?'

The officer could make out the truth from the way Shetty was avoiding his piercing stare.

'Parameshwarayya and Herambha Hegde have received theirs, Saar.'

'What about this person?'

'No, Saar.' Shetty began to perspire.

'Why? He didn't bribe you enough, perhaps, the poor man.'

The officer had rapped him gently but Shetty felt he had been slapped with a slipper at the crossroads. He stood with his head bowed.

'What happened to his case, Shetty?'

'His ... his file is ... missing ... lost, Sir.'

'Oho, so that's how it is, is it?'

The officer looked at Ganapayya. He felt bad. He could not bear to see the farmers suffer in so many new unreasonable ways for no sin of theirs.

'Look here, mister. I'll take the responsibility of settling your dues as soon as the monsoon is over. Don't get frightened. Even if Hosamanehalli is marooned, the water will subside after the rains. You go home now.'

He spoke so gently that Ganapayya could do nothing but leave the place. As he crossed the threshold he could hear the officer taking Shetty to task. He felt relieved.

Ganapayya caught a bus to Aralagodu and from there took a bylane to Hosamane. It was certain now that his connection to his village had not yet been severed.

'Let's see what happens', he said to himself as he trod the familiar pathway. In the distance he could see dark clouds massing over the brow of Sita Parvatha.

Rohini

On this bank of the Sharavathi was the row of Hosamane fields. They were sprawled all over the sloping back of Sita Parvatha. Parameshwarayya's lands in the distance looked uncared for; unkempt with weeds and shrubs.

It was six months since his areca farm had been razed to the ground. Some minister was visiting some place in Sagara and so all the areca palms on his land were chopped off and taken away to decorate the place.

Tender green finger-long seedlings of paddy were standing in Ganapayya's fields. So also in Herambha's. Right in the middle was Ganapayya's house and beyond the fields was Herambha's extensive areca farm. And beyond that, as far as the eye could see, was what used to be Parameshwarayya's areca farm, once flourishing, now desolate. To one side of the areca farms had stood the houses of the labourers, Byra and Hala before they were dismantled and taken away.

Now there was only one house standing, Ganapayya's, the only house in Hosamanehalli.

When Ganapayya was on his way back home after seeing to a few jobs on the farm, he saw Nagaveni walking towards the farm. By the time he washed his hands and feet in the pond and came towards the bund, she was close enough....

'You know, Belli hasn't come home at all.'

Nagaveni always addressed him as 'you know'. The expression signalled that she was talking to him.

'Really?' Ganapayya asked her in the same anxious tone of voice she had used.

A shy blush mingled with the tension on her face.

'Shee ... Is this any time to joke?'

The evening sun had spread lazily over the fields, making the greenery a translucent yellow. Nagaveni too looked delicate as if sprouting tender green leaves like everything else around them. Ganapayya caught his breath with the tightness of hunger, of desire. He stood transfixed.

'You know, did you hear me? Belli hasn't come home yet.'

'I heard you. That's why I said "Really?" didn't I?'

'Yes, she hasn't come home yet,' repeated Nagaveni lamely.

'The bull from the Gowda's cart had come this way while he was collecting sand from the river bed. She might've gone after him.'

'Sheee ...!' said Nagaveni.

Ganapayya cast a glance all over the farm. It was quite some time since the farm hands from Aralagodu had left. There was no one around. Father was not the sort to stir out of the house. And, anyway, why would anyone else come this far?

As Nagaveni looked lost, looking around for Belli, Ganapayya darted towards her and grabbed her.

'Ayyo, let go, let go of me!' she cried, struggling to break free but he hugged her tender body to his own, kissed her cheek and groaned, 'Naaguu!'

Nagaveni slipped out of his embrace and ran ahead of him.

'What is this child's play?' she said as she came out of the farm. Ganapayya followed her.

'She may be grazing on the hill,' he said, 'I'll look for Belli and bring her. You go on – go home.'

But Nagaveni did not go home. 'Come, let's go. I'll come along with you,' she said instead.

The two of them climbed the hillock.

This was the fourth time they had walked up Sita Parvatha together. Soon after they had got married, Ganapayya had taken Nagaveni right up to the cavern and had shown her Sita-Rama's bed. The second time was when Krishnayya had come. And the third time was when Belli had calved in the cave. In the three years since Nagaveni had entered his life, this was the fourth time they were climbing the Parvatha that lay behind their house.

Ganapayya did not often go right up to the crest of the hill. There was no need to. He could get all the firewood they needed from the trees on the slope. If he had to go that far, it had to be under unusual circumstances, like this one when cows or calves strayed away. But even then, he did not always have to go all the way to the top. Quite often such stray cattle could be found in the meadows below or in the jungles of Aralagodu. Very rarely did they go that far. Only Belli was used to climbing all the way up. She had calved in the cave once. Could she have gone up there again?

Ganapayya walked up a winding path on the back of the mountain. Nagaveni followed him, calling out, 'Belli! Belli!' from time to time. He turned back and laughed at her strangely.

'What's so funny, you know?' she asked.

'Woman, I told you I'd look for Belli, didn't I? Why are you coming after me like the tail behind a bull?'

'A bull or a bison. Do I have to teach you to talk? It's been a long time since I've been up the Parvatha. That's why I'm coming with you.'

'Okay, come. But if there's a tiger up there, don't expect me to protect you.'

'Oho, a tiger, is it? You're a big tiger yourself. Can there be another?'

As she giggled tantalizingly, Ganapayya stretched out his hand towards her. She leaned towards him and the two of them walked briskly together in the enveloping twilight.

The view from Sita Parvatha was clear; they could see some three to four miles all around. The Sharavathi had spread out quite a bit to one side. The Linganamakki Dam stood as if it held three or four hills in its embrace. Nestling against the dam was a huge expanse of water lying like the sea amidst forests and ravines. One edge of this body of water had stretched itself right against the foot of the hillock on which they were standing. Beyond the other edge was forestland on low-lying hills and beyond that, in the distance, was a faint glimmer of light. To a side rose a spiral of smoke; from a forest fire, perhaps. The horizon was a trail of reddish streaks against grey skies, left behind by the setting sun.

When Nagaveni went into the cave, calling out to Belli and stretched herself on Sita-Rama's bed, Ganapayya too lay down beside her and kissed her lips. Belli, who had been grazing somewhere behind the cavern, heard her mistress through the boulders, came and stood at the entrance and responded, '*ambaa*'. Ganapayya was aware of her only when she called the second time. He disentangled himself from Nagaveni's embrace, sat up, and threw a stone at her shouting, '*Thu*! You harlot of a cow! Go home!'

And Belli promptly turned homewards.

Nagaveni's rigid body slackened slowly. She rearranged her pallu over her shoulder and sat up, trying to still her heaving breath. The forest fire had burnt itself out, leaving a dull bluish haze in the distance. The open mouth of the empty cave looked grotesque as she left the still warm Sita-Rama's bed and walked over to her husband who stood outside with his back to the cave. As they walked back in silence a wild fowl set up a continuous raucous call.

***

Duggajja sat on the parapet just beyond the thatched awning. The farm hands who had completed the day's work came to him, asking, 'Odeya, can we go home now?' And they had gone back to Aralagodu.

'The *sose* went towards the farm quite some time ago grumbling that Belli hadn't come home. And there's no sign of her since then. Could my *maga* and sose have gone together looking for Belli? Can't they come back soon? It's getting dark. Where could they've gone?' the old man wondered.

He tried to walk a few steps leaning on his stick but felt unsteady. It seemed an effort to lift each foot and put it forward. He went back to the entrance and sat reminiscing. There was a time when he could walk all over Hosamanehalli not once but a thousand times. He was just a stripling when his father had started to farm the land but he could work with his parents shoulder to shoulder. He had sown areca and banana saplings, weeded the land, tied areca sheaths around the fronds to protect the nuts and then he had climbed trees, cut down nuts, peeled them, and stored them in neat piles. His father used to put his arm over his shoulders and say, 'Having this one boy to work with me is like having a hundred farm hands.'

Even in those days, there were not many houses in Hosamanehalli, only four – Herambha Hegde's, his labourer, Byra's, Parameshwarayya's, and his own. Parameshwarayya had not yet become wealthy enough to own a bonded labourer. All these men were still young, barely eight or ten years older than Ganapayya. His father and Herambha's father, Subbaraya, were the only elders in those days. His father died early. Subbaraya lived to a ripe old age; right until people started saying among themselves, 'This old man has no death'. He had died recently. He could easily have been a hundred years when he died.

Duggajja wondered how old he himself was. Sixty, perhaps. But he felt like an old man, wasting away with illness. Now that his son had got him some medicine from Sagara for his cough and wheezing, he was a little better than he used to be. But whenever the rains came he was confined to bed. It was ten to fifteen years since he had started this dreadful wheezing. He had tried every herbal concoction but nothing had helped.

The old man sat still. A cool breeze wafted in from the farm. The hillock behind the house and farm cast a deep shadow on them. The birds had stopped chirping. A few clouds were drifting in the darkening sky. Only the water from the pond in the farm was flowing lazily. The old man looked all around him. As he saw Herambha's farm and the walls of his dismantled house, fear clutched at his heart.

'What a fate for an innocent village!' the old man grieved, 'Just four to five families; a few people with their joys and pain. We had everything here. But now, all we have is barrenness. It wasn't as if this village had people spilling over, bustling with excitement as on the main street in Talaguppa town. It was always like this, quiet and restful with hardly any people about. But there was the security of neighbourliness, a feeling that if I called out to Herambha or Prameshwarayya, one or the other would come; a certainty that Byra and Hala were somewhere around the place.

'Now, who can I call? If I shout "Coo", will it reach Aralagodu or Bheemeshwara? Will those people heed my call and come all this way? And if things are so bad now, how will it be once the rains come and this place is covered with water? We may not even get labourers to work on the farm and the field. How much can my family do? I must tell Ganapa to see if we can get some men here before the monsoon. We've decided to stay on for this year for better, for worse, whether it's wise or not. But there's always the fear of what might happen after that.'

Belli came ambling down the hill and made her way towards the back of the house.

'The cow is home.... Where did these two go?'

As the old man peered into the distance, he saw his son emerging from the darkness. And behind him was the daughter-in-law.

'Koose, Belli's gone to the backyard,' the old man called out to her. She did not respond but rushed into the house.

Ganapayya sat beside his father and told him how Belli had gone right up the hillock, how he and his wife had gone there looking for her and had brought her back. It was pitch dark by the time he finished his story. Nagaveni lit a lamp and placed it on the platform.

During dinner they talked of getting some farm hands to stay with them throughout the monsoon. Herambha had suggested that Ganapayya should get a few Nayak men from the Deevru community as the regular daily-wage labourers from Aralagodu were not willing to stay on the land. They resented the extra work, of course, but they were also afraid of what might happen to the village during the rains. They would have to look after Herambha's field and farm besides Ganappaya's. Once water surrounded the hillock they would probably not be able to get extra labour. Ganapayya might get one or two men for the season. But planting rice seedlings and sheathing the arecanut fronds would need more than three or four people even if Ganapayya and his wife joined them. That was why the men from Aralagodu had refused to stay.

'Right now, we could do with a man and a woman', said Duggajja, 'and later on we could get a few more, can't we?'

'Why shouldn't we bring a Deevru or a Hasalaru family?' thought Ganapayya. 'If we provide them with house, food, and clothes, they might stay the five months. They can go back when we move on.' And turning to his father, he said, 'I'll go to Talaguppa tomorrow. Let's see.'

After the old man finished his dinner and went outside, Nagaveni asked her husband while serving him, 'You know, are you going to Talaguppa tomorrow?'

'Yes. Why?'

'I was just wondering ... It's so long since I've seen Amma.... Once the rains come we won't be able to stir out of the house....'

Nagaveni's mother's house was quite close to Talaguppa. She had been there last during the Bellaane temple fair. And she had never visited her family again. They had sent word asking her to go over but how could she unless her husband sent her?

'Appayya will be alone in the house ...'

Yes, that was a problem. Was it wise to leave an ailing old man alone and go? Nagaveni stared at her husband's face to see if he would think of a way out.

'Let's take the ten o'clock Gajanana bus and return as quickly as possible. Appayya may not mind staying alone for those few hours.'

Nagaveni nodded happily.

Previously, the distance from Hosamanehalli to Talaguppa was a mere six miles, from Hosamane to Hiremane and thence to Talaguppa. All they had to do was cross the Sharavathi. But now it was twenty miles. Since the old road was submerged, they had to get to Aralagodu, go to Kargal from there, and then to Talaguppa. Where they used to pay eight annas previously, they now paid a rupee and eight. Where they once took half an hour to cover the distance, they now took an hour and a half.

Dugajja was quite willing to send his son and daughter-in-law off on a mission to get farm hands who would stay with them through the monsoon. They told the daily-wage labourers to sheath the arecanuts, had an early lunch, and set off.

'Get red chillies, dhall, and other such groceries. Anyway, the monsoon will be here,' Dugajja reminded his son.

'Yes, I will,' replied Ganapayya as he walked away with his wife.

'Will the water come all this way?' Nagaveni asked her husband as they set their backs to the hillock and walked on. They took the road from Hosamane to Aralagodu. Though it was on an elevation, the government officials had planted red stones all the way to show how high the water would reach when the dam was done.

'Not this year, perhaps', Ganapayya replied, adding, 'if it doesn't rise this high we shouldn't have any problems. People will still be able to come here and we'll be able to go out. But how can we be absolutely sure it won't? What guarantee is there in what the government says? Anyway, if the water does rise, we'll be in trouble. We'll be stranded until it goes down again.'

Nagaveni was not unduly perturbed. She was happy with the thoughts of visiting her mother's house. There was a spring in her step and laughter in her voice. Her face was suffused with a glow which made her so attractive that Ganapayya felt a special tenderness towards her.

They crossed the bridge, walked past Aithumane, and reached Aralagodu in time for the bus. It was small, old, and rickety. The commuters were crammed like pickled lime but the conductor did not want to leave anyone behind. So Ganapayya and Nagaveni got in.

And the bus lumbered past place names etched on stone slabs – Kargal, Idavani, Bachagaru, Talavata, Hiremane.... People who had to get down got down and those who wanted to get in got in. By the time it reached Talaguppa, the sky was overcast and the wind fearsome. Ganapayya was looking for someone familiar with whom he could send Nagaveni to her mother's house when she called out to him, 'You know, isn't that Krishnayya?'

Krishnayya came running up to them with, 'Bava, how is it you're here? And how're you, Nagu?' he said.

'Nagu, come back here by five. I'll be waiting for you,' said Ganapayya.

Nagaveni nodded.

'Why don't you come with us, Bava?' asked Krishnayya.

'I've got to see to something else,' replied Ganapayya and walked away towards Bhatta's shop.

By the time Nagaveni and Krishnayya crossed the railway track and walked towards their house, the wind became gusty. There was a cloud-burst; lightning shattered the sky, bringing down a thunder shower. Krishnayya opened his umbrella and held it towards Nagaveni but she took a few moments to move under it. Even when she walked beside him, she held herself together in the heavy rain.

Krishnayya had grown up in Nagaveni's house. He was ten years older than her. Nagaveni's father had brought him to work in the house but had raised him like a member of the family. He was Krishnayya to Nagaveni. Her husband was Bava to Krishnayya, a brother-in-law.

Krishnayya was tall and fair, a strapping young man. Not just that. He had a luxuriant moustache on his broad face. He was friendly. Everyone in his neighbourhood was familiar with his winsome smile. And he had the zest to do the work of ten people.

Nagaveni was fond of·him. She was always happy in his presence, whether listening to his stories or watching him at work. He too felt the same way towards her.

When Nagaveni got married and left for her husband's house, it was Krishnayya who had wept the most. People said he had not eaten for three days. He had gone right up to Talaguppa to see her off.

'Nagu, I'll go back now. You go on to your husband's house,' he had said. And she had wept her heart out. Only she knew she was crying for him. The others thought it was but natural for a bride to weep when she left her mother's house for the first time. Of course, she had also wept to go away to a strange house. But then, she needed a reason to cope with the ache in her heart, didn't she?

The rain became torrential and while Nagaveni was drenched on one side of the umbrella, Krishnayya was soaked on the other. Somehow they reached home under that one umbrella.

Nagaveni spent a few hours with her parents, brothers, and younger sister.

'Stay on,' said her mother as she was leaving.

'No, Amma. He wants us to get back this evening,' replied Nagaveni and bid everyone goodbye.

Krishnayya went along with her to the bus stand.

The thunderstorm had passed. The trees looked fresh and vibrant in the dull sunlight. The sky was washed clean and blue. Water stood everywhere in little puddles, glistening. The rice fields were green with shoots of paddy.

'Are you going far away, Nagu?'

'Not now. After the rains. They've given land and money to everyone else in our village. Everyone but us. We're the only family in Hosamane now.'

'Really?'

'Yes. That's why he's come to Talaguppa to look for labourers who'll stay and work the land with us throughout the rains.'

'Shall I come?'

'Come.'

'I can come right away. Feed me two meals a day and I'll do the work of ten people.'

Nagaveni looked up at him and laughed.

Ganapayya was waiting for them. Krishnayya helped in loading the bag of groceries on top of the bus. Nagaveni's face looked pinched as the bus moved. Krishnayya waved at them as they sped away.

'Were you able to get someone to stay with us?' Nagaveni asked her husband as they walked towards their village.

'No. It doesn't look as if we can get anyone. I asked everywhere, in Talaguppa, Manamane, and Marthuru. No one's willing to come.... Don't know what we should do.... It would've been good to have someone now that the rain's upon us. How can we live on our own here?'

Nagaveni walked silently, a little ahead of her husband.

'Perhaps our Krishnayya would come if we asked him,' she said, turning towards him.

'Krishnayya? Yes, maybe we could ask him. But who'll see to the work there, at your father's house?'

'There'll always be someone there. Deevru farm hands are easy to get in that place. Send word to Krishnayya tomorrow or the day after. Let him come.'

'Let's do that.'

It was dusk by the time they passed Aithumane and came to the bridge. It had rained heavily. There was water everywhere – a sure sign the monsoon had set in. The Rohini rains had been coming on and off the past four days. The saplings in the fields stood with their heads held high. The land that had shrivelled up in the sun was now wet and pliant. Some farmers had started to plough and sow. Heavy wind, thunder, and lightning were harbingers of the *mirugi* phase of the monsoon. Once this intermittent rain became incessant, it would stop only after four months. Ganapayya had to stock up everything they needed and chop more firewood. He had to repair the farmhouse; it needed a new thatch. There were quite a few things to be seen to.

'I'd better send for Krishnayya tomorrow,' he said to himself.

They could see the burning lamp on the platform.

'O, Appayya's got up and lit the lamp. Poor old man!' said Ganapayya.

Even as they neared the house, he heard his soft voice, 'Maani?'

'We're here,' he said as they stepped into the awning at the door.

Mrigashira

It was the feast of the Mirugi rain and so none of the farm hands had come to work that day. The first phase of work on the farm had been completed anyway. Only the thatch roof on the farmhouse had to be repaired. All it needed was a few bundles of hay set firmly in the patchy places. That too could have been done but then the labourers had not turned up.

For the past eight days, the rain had not let up; the dark clouds had not stirred. Nothing could be seen except a blinding sheet of rain. Nothing could be heard except its deafening *rapa-rapa*. It poured without a moment's respite, the onslaught causing the roof of the farmhouse to leak in many places. The workers must have thatched it badly in the first place because the floor was covered with water.

The previous night, the rain had been simpering a bit but had settled down to a self-assured drizzle early that morning; the clouds looked as grouchy as ever. This was the right time to repair the roof but the men had not come. They had to celebrate their Mirugi *habba*.

Ganapayya had heard the drumbeats from beyond the farm since the previous night. He went out alone towards the areca palms. Even as he walked down the slope, he saw the Sharavathi. Previously, before the dam had risen, the rivers flow was towards the waterfall. Now he could see the water but not the flow. With the dam blocking its way it had stopped right there beside their hillock, restless and choppy. Just the previous week he could see the tips of the boulders on the hill. The water had not risen much. But now it had widened the riverbed on the side away from the hill and was threatening to overflow the bank. The Sharavathi lay like a pregnant woman, full and ready for birthing.

The workers who had come the previous day had said that water stood on the other side of the hill. So it seemed certain that it would surround the hill as the monsoon progressed. After that, no one would be able to venture this way. It was eight days since Krishnayya had sent word that he would be coming. Why had he not come? It would be good if he came before Hosamanehalli became an island.

A lime tree floated, wrenched out by its roots. A few banana plants too had met with the same fate. The water in the pond had eroded a part of the bund to the farm and so one of the areca palms was in danger of falling. As Ganapayya crossed the bridge and turned towards the house, he heard someone calling him. He turned to see Krishnayya.

'Oho! Come, come....'

Krishnayya jumped down from the farmlands to the bridge which shook a bit under his weight.

'Bavayya, did you think I wasn't coming?' he asked.

Ganapayya noticed Krishnayya's attractive moustache and felt a twinge of envy.

'Naturally! Arre, when did you send word you were coming? And why have you taken so long?'

'What could I do, Bava? I was all set to come here eight days ago but Yajamanaru wanted me to see to something in Sagara. I thought that job would take me two days. But it took eight. Anyway, I'm glad I could come at least today. Or else I would've had to swim to your village from the Aralagodu bridge.'

'Why?'

'Don't you know? The Sharavathi is girdling your village from either side. In another four days Hosamanehalli will become an island.'

'Really? Has water risen behind the mountain?'

'Yes Bava. The water's rising from both the sides of the hill. The walkway to Aralagodu isn't covered yet only because it's on a higher level. If the water keeps rising like this, even that pathway will be flooded.'

'Hmm ... just as I feared! Did you go to the house before coming here?'

'No, Bava, I saw you walking towards the farm and so I came here right away.'

'Come, let's go home. She's been waiting for you since these eight days.'

Ganapayya walked up the valley with Krishnayya. A few stray sunbeams peeped weakly from behind the clouds.

Nagaveni had been cleaning rice in a winnowing-fan. But instead of throwing away the paddy she was throwing away grains of rice absent-mindedly. And then, looking at the white grains of rice on the black floor she scolded herself, 'Thu, what's got into me?' and picked up all the rice grains she could and put them back.

These days she was bored in Hosamane. Fortunately for her, her father-in-law kept her company. Or else being in the house would have become tedious. Working on the farm and field had lost its charm as she had to work alone like an owl. Of course, Ganapayya worked alongside. He did say a word or two. But even then, it was not like working together with a group of people. There was a feeling of isolation now. Her husband was taciturn by nature. He spoke only when he was in the mood, not otherwise. And even when he did, there was no intimacy, no companionship she could bank on. It was just so much and not anymore. She was never quite sure if it was sheer indifference or a real contempt that made him keep his distance from her.

Earlier someone or the other would visit them. Herambha's wife or Prameshwarayya's wife would come and talk about this, that, or the other. The Hasalaru women would stand beyond the back door or near the awning and talk about things happening in their lives. Now all of them had gone away. The Deervu women from Aralagodu had not come that way for ages now. At least if they had come, Nagamani would have felt there were some people around. But now she was oppressed by a sense of loneliness.

'It's eight days since Krishnayya sent word to say he's coming,' she thought, 'and he hasn't come yet. I waited for him today, hoping he'd be here. If he comes, I can at least get some news from home. And I won't feel so lonely either. We've grown up together after all. If he comes, I'll surely be rid of this maddening boredom.'

Nagaveni finished cleaning the rice. She put it away and went into the bathroom. Water was flowing with a melodious *julu-julu* into the cauldron from the drain cut out of areca stems. She took water in a *chembu*, tucked her sari a little higher, washed her feet, and came inside the house.

'Koose!' called her father-in-law from the platform outside the front door, 'Who's that talking?'

Nagaveni stiffened. Previously there was no need for such questions. Where there was a village, there had to be people coming and going and talking. Not only the people who lived in it, sometimes those who had to cross the Sharavathi went past the house. Farm hands from Aralagodu too went by on their way to and from work. But now there was dread hovering about, a fear of strangers in the vicinity and questions like 'Who?' 'Why?' entered the head.

When Nagaveni came to the front door and strained her ears towards the voices, she discerned Krishnayya's louder voice even before her husband's.

'Looks like Krishnayya's come, Mava,' she said. And as soon as she was sure it was him, she darted beyond the awning to see him cross the bridge. Krishnayya saw her and waved. The tender leaves of a pepper creeper fluttered coquettishly in the breeze.

'I thought you'd never come,' she said as he climbed the steps to the open veranda. 'Is everyone well at home?'

Krishnayya laughed his loud laugh, put his bag on the platform beside the old man, and brought his palms together to greet Duggajja with a namaskara.

'Thatha, how're you? How's your health now?' he asked the old man in his deep voice.

'As well as I can be. My wheezing's no better. The rains scare me. But tell me, how's everyone at home?'

'They're well, Thatha. Yajamanaru thinks of you quite often. He says you should be taken to Talaguppa or Sagara. He feels medicines from those towns could make you better.'

'Doctors and medicines are just illusions, like smearing oil on a tree with wood-rot. Will a lifespan that's moving forwards ever run backwards?' Then turning to his daughter-in-law who was gawking at Krishnayya, Duggajja said, 'Koose, you're just standing there ... go, bring him some water.'

Nagaveni brought him water to wash his feet before entering the house.

'Krishnayya, go and have a bath,' said Ganapayya, coming from inside. Krishnayya took a panche from his bag and went into the house.

'How's the pain in Amma's waist?' Nagaveni asked, stopping him near the kitchen as he was going to the bathroom.

'She seems to be a little better now. The vaidya from Talaguppa had given her some herbal oil. Massaging with it seems to have helped.'

Nagaveni had not forgotten that her mother had said her lower-back was stiff with pain.

'Has Nagaraja come home?' Nagaraja was her younger brother. He was doing his High School in Sagara.

'No', shouted Krishnayya from the bathroom, 'He may come next week.'

As she heard the water splashing off his back, Nagaveni turned her attention to the smoky fireplace.

'Is dinner ready?' asked Ganapayya, coming into the kitchen.

'The curry is ready. I've got to cook rice. Couldn't you have brought four banana leaves as you were coming in from the farm? We don't have any on which to serve dinner.'

'Did you tell me to get some? Or did I have to dream that you didn't have any?'

'So what? You can get some now, can't you?'

'Oho, I can get some, of course ... as if I'm a servant in her father's house to get some....'

The fire lit up suddenly and Ganapayya moved back with a start. Nagaveni looked at his face in the glow.

He was not teasing her; he seemed irritated about something.

'Don't worry, Krishnayya will get them,' she said to pacify him.

Ganapayya stalked out of the kitchen, hungry and angry.

Clouds covered the sun but there was no rain. Only the wind blew fiercely and there was the distant sound of thunder. But the clouds were low-lying, a sure sign of rain. After dinner Ganapayya took Krishnayya and went out of the house. He had not forgotten what Krishnayya had told him; that Sharavathi was tightening her grip around the Parvatha. Only the road to Aralagodu might be spared.

Ganapayya was frightened that this road too would be engulfed. They should be starting on the next phase of work in the fields and on the farms. What if the labourers from Aralagodu could not come?

Ganapayya walked with Krishnayya along the path to Aralagodu. When they climbed the hillock from one side and went over to the other, they could see the river. It had never come this far. Previously, Sharavathi would flow, hugging a side of the mountain, never straying from her path. But now that her flow was blocked further down, she had begun to spread out, encroaching the neighbouring forest and valley. Trees, shrubs, and bamboo were already knee-deep in rain water, in red muddy water, still and silent.

Ganapayya looked at Krishnayya.

'See how high the water has risen in the past three days. There's no doubt the Parvatha will be marooned in the next three. It'll become an island. And then?'

'Don't worry, Bavayya, I'll see to the work on the field and farm. You don't worry about anything....'

'Who ever thought the government would bring us to this state, Ayya? They've sent everyone else from this village to other places compensating them substantially. But they didn't do anything in my case.... To whom can I now go and talk about our troubles?'

Ganapayya grumbled as if to himself.

'Come, Bavayya, let's go home. It looks like rain.'

Krishnayya took Ganapayya home. The rain was virtually on their heels as they stepped onto the veranda.

That rain poured continuously for eight days.

Aridhraa

'Survive the Aridhraa, you're sure of a harvest'; the proverb kept running in Krishnayya's head as he walked back from Aralagodu. As if the Mirugi rain was not enough, the Aridhraa came pelting down. It was almost impossible to get labourers from Aralagodu to work on the farm. Herambha's seedlings had to be planted. Ganapayya had seeded his fields directly to save the bother of transplanting. But then, his fields had to be weeded. And palm sheaths had to be tied around the arecanut fronds. Though Krishnayya was willing to see to everything, Ganapayya had insisted that they should get help from Aralagodu.

The Sharavathi had already begun to engulf Sita Parvatha but had spared the pathway to Aralagodu. As there was a bulge behind the hillock attached to the Aralagodu hill, water had yet to rise at least five to six feet before it could cover it. So the road from Hosamane to Aralagodu was safe even though expanses of water had formed deep pools on either side of it. Taking advantage of the accessibility, Ganapayya got men from Aralagodu and hastily got the work on the farm and field done. But it was not easy; it took all his patience to cajole them to walk through the rising water to Hosamane. They finally consented only when he raised their wages by eight annas per day.

By the time the fields were weeded, Duggajja was unable to rise from his bed. The wheezing worsened day by day. The old man was hardly aware of what was happening around him. All they could hear was a groan or two from time to time. His condition deteriorated further. Krishnayya went to Aralagodu and got some herbal medicine from a local doctor. Nothing worked. As the Aridhraa rain entered its third phase, Duggajja breathed his last.

Krishnayya went out to see if he could find someone through whom he could send word to others but he had to turn back halfway. The deluge that had forced her way through the Sharavathi was now roaring around Sita Parvatha.

They cremated the old man in front of the cave atop the hill. Ganapayya lit the funeral pyre in a fine drizzle. Krishnayya stood to one side with his arms folded. Nagaveni stood behind him. The rain stopped as the pyre caught fire and waited until it burnt itself down to ashes. It started only when the three turned their backs to the cave and wended their way back home.

The land had become indifferent to the monsoon. Only the pouring rain and the sweeping wind had life in them. Everything else crouched in fear of the ravaging downpour like the bald boulders on the crest of Sita Parvatha. The saplings in the fields stood breathing in the water as it flowed from field to field to join the river. They were barely as tall as a span as they shivered in the onslaught of wind and rain, yet they stood breathing in the slush.

The first sacrifice to the fury of the monsoon was the areca farm. The palms and the banana leaves took the force of the pelting raindrops. The palms that tore away from the trunk with the onslaught of every gust of wind, the trees that came crashing down with them, the pepper creepers that had relied on the tree trunks and the leaves floating in water, everything spoke of the havoc the rains were spreading. Amidst this death, only the pond was rejuvenated. It had been sighing with suffocation during the summer but was now gurgling with laughter, returning water to the Sharavathi a hundredfold.

Water was cascading in torrents from Sita Parvatha too. The steady trickle of rainwater from the roof was all that could be collected for Ganapayya's bathroom as the spring in the hill was now a pond and there were a hundred rivulets streaming out of this pond. All the water headed towards the river.

The Sharavathi was swelling by the moment. Parameshwarayya's lands, hugging a bank, were already inundated. Herambha's lands were not very far away from the river; barely the distance between the outstretched arms of ten men. If the water rose any further, it was quite likely that the water from the river would rush into his field instead of the other way around.

Water had encircled Sita Parvatha. From a distance, Hosamanehalli looked like an island, like an insignificant rock in the sea, a helpless piece of land surrounded by a watery girdle with no contact with the outside world whatsoever.

Parameshwarayya's lands were under water. His house and the house of his labourer, Hala, had caved in, waiting to be washed away. Even Herambha's house and his Byra's house were on their way to desolation. The only things standing were Herambha's and Ganapayya's lands and Ganapayya's house was the only house.

And all it contained was the thatched awning; the veranda with a platform to one side, two dark cave-like rooms, a kitchen, an open bathroom at the back, a cowshed, a shack to stock wood, Ganapayya, on the veranda leaning against the wall, Krishnayya seated on the floor, leaning against a pillar, and Nagaveni walking in and out of the house seeing to her chores. The last three were the only people in Hosamanehalli.

Krishnayya got up and walked down the veranda along the edge of the thatched roof to keep from getting wet. He went to a side and spat out the betel leaf and nut he was chewing. He stood a while watching its red mingle with the brown of the muddy water, and hoisting his maunji over his panche, returned to sit against the pillar in the veranda and faced Ganapayya.

'Bavayya, when do the new rains start? From this Sunday?'

'It's eleven days since the Aridhraa rains began, isn't it? Yes, Punarvasu is from Sunday. But let's see if it brings its rain or not.'

'I only hope it'll give us some respite. How does it expect people to survive this onslaught? Shouldn't we get some rest, day or night?' Krishnayya picked up a small twig and talked, cleaning his teeth.

'Ayyo, let the rain be, Maaraaya. It's that cursed dam!' Ganapayya snapped, 'What shall we do if the stagnating water doesn't sink? We're caught here, aren't we? Suppose something happens to us, what'll be our fate?'

'We're our only help, Bavayya. Either we make a raft or we swim across.'

'I really don't know what to do.'

Ganapayya sat with his head in his hands. He was weighed down with worries he could not handle. He had never felt so helpless ever before. His spirit trembled every time it struck him afresh that they were not in touch with the world outside.

The water in the river had to subside someday, if not today or tomorrow. There was enough to eat for the next four to five months. Work on the lands was done. The two of them could see to the odds and ends; they did not need help from Aralagodu. The fear was not for any of these reasons. It was only because water had surrounded them and isolated them from the rest of the world.

Whenever water stood in the neighbouring forests and valleys during monsoon, wild animals would come towards Sita Parvatha, seeking refuge. And now foxes, deer, and wild goats strolled fearlessly behind the house looking for shelter. A python crept into the wood-shack beside the kitchen. Rabbits scurried about the veranda. The cattle had mooed restlessly a few nights earlier. Nagaveni said she had heard the low oomphs and coughs of a tiger near the cattleshed before dawn. She could be right; perhaps that was why the cattle were restive. Wild animals like the tiger, cheetah, bison, and wild boar lived in the Malenadu forests but they lived in their own territory most of the time. Now with all the extra water around they could be scared too. Ganapayya became even more apprehensive because of their presence. A tiger entered Ganapayya's heart as he sat with his head in his hands.

'Krishnayya, do you know – Nagu heard a tiger roaring near the cattleshed?' he said, turning towards him.

'Really? When?'

'Early this morning. Last night the cows and calves were mooing. They must've seen the tiger.'

Nagaveni had come outside to do something but stood there on hearing talk about the tiger.

'You know, Krishnayya, there's a tiger on the prowl, that's for sure. I heard it clearly this morning.'

'From which side did you hear it?'

'From the back of the house. There's one in the jungles of Hidamba. The farm hands from Alaragodu used to talk about a tiger in that area. Couldn't that same tiger have come here, now that its forest is drowned?'

'Yes, Bavayya, what she says could be true. That tiger could have come this way for protection. We've got to be careful. If it's eyeing our cattleshed, it means danger is lurking very near. Tonight we must secure the door of the shed firmly.'

'Yes, we should.'

'Bavayya, don't you have a gun?'

'No, Maaraaya, I don't. Herambha had one. I didn't keep any. Maybe I should've got one too.'

'Krishnayya, do you know how to shoot?' This was from Nagaveni. She was curious. She had never seen him handling a gun. How did he get to learn anything at all about it?

'I? I learnt quite recently. Padavagoud Basappa taught me. I even shot him a wild boar as *gurudakshine*!'

Nagaveni laughed.

'We could've taken care of the tiger too ... if only we had a gun', Krishnayya said softly as if speaking to himself, 'we've got to be wary.'

That night Krishnayya himself went and locked the door of the cattle shed. It was quite some time since Ganapayya had had his dinner and had gone to bed. The lamp shone faintly on the dividing wall between the rooms. Black soot covered the top half of the chimney like a crown and the wall near the chimney too had a black streak. As Krishnayya got his blanket and settled down to sleep, Nagaveni came out after finishing her chores in the kitchen.

'Sleepy, Krishnayya?'

'How can I be sleepy this early? ... Are you done for the day?'

'Done!'

Wiping her hands on the pallu of her sari, Nagaveni went inside. Then she came out. Her husband was snoring. She sat on the threshold and drew the plate of betel leaves and nuts towards her.

'Want to chew?' she asked.

'No, my eyes are burning.' Krishnayya yawned as he sat leaning against a wall.

Nagaveni tossed a betel nut into her mouth, clipped the stalk of a betel leaf, smeared some sunna on it, and started chewing it.

'Wonder which *raavu* has got hold of this rain!' she exclaimed vehemently.

The rain was unrelenting. And besides, there was the wind. The Aridhraa rains poured without a pause. They had hoped Aridhraa would be mild since Mrigashira had been virulent, but there was no sign of it diminishing. In fact, Aridhraa seemed to be competing with Mrigashira with a will to win.

'Why? Shouldn't it rain during the rainy season? Is the sun supposed to shine? As long as the water doesn't rise till here and drown the village, we're safe,' Krishnayya countered.

'Who knows what'll happen, Krishnayya? I told him, "Let's not worry about the compensation from the government. We'll think about it later. For now, let's get away from here." But he wouldn't listen to me. Mava too didn't want us to move out. Appayya wouldn't have said anything if we'd spent these four months with them. He could've gone to the office a few more times, seen this man and that, and had got the money and lands due to us. But he'll do only what *he* wants to do. Somebody told him the village wouldn't drown this year. And so he decided we should stay on. Mava died here. That was his wish, anyway. Who knows what else is awaiting us? Tigers, foxes, snakes, and boars have started living behind our house.'

Krishnayya could not bear the heaviness in Nagaveni's voice. And yet he could understand her husband's pig-headedness. He knew how Ganapayya felt about moving in with his father-in-law even if it was for a mere four months. He had spoken to Krishnayya about the delicacy of the situation. Also, he was not sure if the government would really compensate him after the monsoon. If he left the saplings he had planted and went to live with his wife's family, what would they eat later? And if the government let him down, would he have to live on his father-in-law's bounty for a year? This was Ganapayya's unspoken fear. But how could a woman like Nagaveni understand all this?

Krishnayya got up from where he was sitting and went forward. When Nagaveni pushed the plate of betel leaves and nuts towards him he took it and sat down.

'What's the point in weeping now, Nagu?' he said, 'Bavayya didn't want to throw away the morsel of food in his hand. And so he's stayed on. What can we do about it now? Yes, there's water surrounding the village. But can we move from here? We have to stay and face whatever comes, shouldn't we? Why are you scared? Bavayya's here, I'm here. Be brave.'

'It's easy for you to take his side, Krishnayya. My heart keeps trembling day and night. I'm gripped with so many fears: What will happen when? What if water rushes into the house? What if the tiger or a boar comes in and takes away one of us? Of course, I do feel a little braver because you're here. I'd have died by now if you hadn't come.'

'Ayyo, you silly girl! With two men in the house, will we leave a woman to the tiger?' Krishnayya laughed at her heartily.

Nagaveni sat staring at his reddened lips and his arms and chest heaving with laughter. She felt comforted to hear him; more restful, much like coming to a cool shady place after a long blistering walk in the hot summer sun. She wondered why she found Krishnayya's presence and his chatter so pleasing, so reassuring. Why did she want to keep staring at him, to sit with him? Why did her heart jump with joy whenever she caught sight of him? What could be the reason?

Perhaps the zing of the betel nut had got to her head or the bit of tobacco had made her lightheaded. Nagaveni felt like stretching out right where she was. How nice it would be if Krishnayya were to sit closer and she could rest her head on his lap and go to sleep. 'Previously I used to touch him with such ease, even beat him. I was quite comfortable touching him until I was about twelve-thirteen. Only Amma would tell me it was not the right thing to do. But since I got married Krishnayya's gone far from me; very far....' Her thoughts meandered on.

She felt resentful, agitated. Krishnayya's comforting words made room for other thoughts to surface; thoughts she had never thought before. She wanted to tell him she was not happy here. She wanted to rest her head on his chest and weep. She looked up.

'Get up, Nagu. Go and sleep,' said Krishnayya and going to his bed, he lay down and drew the blanket over his head.

Nagaveni sat on for a while on the threshold, soothing her ruffled emotions and then got up.

'What's come over me? Why are these crazy feelings running through me? Why have I got so fond of Krishnayya lately? How could I've forgotten my husband sleeping in the inner room?'

She got up in a hurry, took the wall lamp and went into the room. She closed the door, bolted it, and hung the lamp on a nail on the wall and turned towards her husband's bed. That was when she was aware of his two red eyes, wide open and staring at her. She felt as if someone had thrown smouldering ember at her.

'Are you done with talking?' The question felt like the sting of a rap on a tethered calf.

'Yes ... why?'

'Just asked ... you could've gone on longer, couldn't you?' Nagaveni put off the lamp and got into bed. As she drew up her blanket to cover her face, she heard Ganapayya's, 'You're going beyond the limit these days.'

Nagaveni was in no mood to talk. She turned over to the other side. The cot creaked. The rats in the granary scampered down. Ganapayya clenched his fists and cleaved the darkness with his stare.

When Nagaveni had come into the room earlier Ganapayya had just finished his first round of sleep. He had expected her to return with the lamp. But she had not come. She had sat with Krishnayya instead, chewing betel leaves with him. And then they got chatting. Though he could not make out what they were talking about because of the rain, Ganapayya was furious that she wanted to talk to him at all.

'This isn't anything new, it was always like this. There was a spring in her step every time we talked about Krishnayya. And she's been moving about the house with a new verve ever since he came to stay. How much she talks to him, how much she laughs with him. Why? Is he her elder brother? He's just an orphan her father brought home and looked after. Where's the need to be so familiar with him? Why?'

He had thought of slapping her as soon as she came in from chatting with Krishnayya. But he controlled himself with great difficulty. After all Nagaveni was his wife. It was not good for him to distrust her so easily. He should wait and see. And so he had swallowed his overflowing wrath and merely said, 'You're going beyond the limit.' But it sounded like a whiplash.

He turned towards her but Nagaveni had deliberately moved farther from him. 'If she can be so insolent, can't I be much more?' he said to himself as he turned away from her.

But for the sound of the wind and rain, there was silence. The cold mountain air from Sita Parvatha breezed through the whole house.

Punarvasu

By the time Saturday evening made way for Sunday morning, the sun was shining brightly. The rain had tucked in all signs of sound and fury and the sky was as clean as a well-swept front yard. Except for a few puddles here and there, the floor started drying in the front porch, the backyard and the awning. Birds flew about in the tender sunlight. Wildfowl and hare scurried about from shrubs and thickets. Sounds of *keech-keech* came from the birds in Sita Parvatha. The cattle, tired of being cooped up in the byre, stretched out their necks and stared at the sun.

Now they were sure the Punarvasu rain would give them an eight-day respite. Krishnayya tightened a girdle round his waist, stuck his knife through it, and went towards the farm. Ganapayya slung a spade over his shoulder and set out towards the fields. Nagaveni felt light-hearted as she went about her work.

The rains had not created much havoc in Ganapayya's farm. There were a few new potholes where water had eroded the bank and had formed small pools. An areca palm that had been teetering for quite some time had fallen. One or two saplings too were washed away and a few banana plants were destroyed. By the time Krishnayya wandered around the farm and came towards the field, Ganapayya was standing on a low ridge and surveying it.

Even here there was no damage to speak of. Water flowed from one field to the other. The shoots were a rich green. They stood in the slush and swayed in the morning breeze that came in gentle waves to tickle them. A gentle sunlight pervaded the field

'How's the farm?' asked Ganapayya.

'Nothing much has happened there, Bava. Remember the areca palm near the bridge? Only *that* has fallen.'

Both of them walked towards Herambha's farm. The wind had wrecked some havoc there. A few trees were uprooted. The water from the pond had gushed into the farm and had washed away the sheaths that protected the fronds. As they trudged towards Herambha's paddy field, Ganapayya groaned, 'Ayyo!' The Sharavathi had forced her way into the field, submerging the low-lying area hugging her bank. But, at least, the rest of the field was safe.

Krishnayya noticed the river water; it was thick and slushy.

'Bavayya, the water won't rise any higher,' he said.

'How can you tell?' asked Ganapayya, staring at him.

'Listen to that noise in the distance. Isn't that the sound of water overflowing from the dam? The wall's about ninety to a hundred feet high now. So, it's holding that much of water and releasing only the rest. Bavayya, we've won the battle!' he exclaimed.

Ganapayya too felt he had won the battle this monsoon.

The Sharavathi was flowing forward in slow motion. So it meant that water would not stagnate in pools. He could let go of the fear that the village would drown.

'Yes, you're right!' Ganapayya nodded.

The two of them walked home in companionable silence, happy they had survived the trial by water.

As they entered the veranda, they saw Nagaveni standing on the platform, crying.

'Krishnayya! ... In the kitchen ... a snake!'

'What? A snake?' Ganapayya stepped back voluntarily.

'Where?' said Krishnayya rushing into the house.

Resting its tail over the threshold to the kitchen was a water-snake, sleeping peacefully. The rest of its body was hidden somewhere in the kitchen.

'Here, hit it! It's not a cobra, Krishnayya. It's just a water-snake,' said Ganapayya bringing a long stick and handing it to him.

Krishnayya pushed him aside, signalled to Nagaveni to move away, and holding the snake by the tail, he twisted it once round his hand and gave it a quick tug. A five feet long snake emerged and hung squirming in his grip. Holding the snake high above his head Krishnayya ran towards the backyard. He swung the snake aloft briskly four times and flung it into the distance. It flew skywards, fell with a splash, slithered, and righted itself. Krishnayya caught hold of it again and tossed it again the same way. The snake fell into the bushes beyond the yard.

Nagaveni threw him an admiring look as she went inside.

After lunch Krishnayya went out for a stroll. He felt tied down with the constant rain. He wanted a long walk in the sun and so took the road from Hosamane to Aralagodu. He walked towards the Sita Parvatha. Because there were hardly any people going up the hill these days, the pathway was covered over with grass; he could not make out the way to the top. He climbed a bit of Sita Parvatha and then got down on the other side. He had scarcely walked ten steps when he saw water. He stopped. It was like a waterfall. There was water everywhere; to the right, to the left, wherever he looked. It had spread out for over a furlong in front of him. And beyond it, in the distance, was the green hill of Aralagodu with its houses and fields. But on this side of the bridge he could see only the top of submerged trees. The water was at least ten feet high. Will this water ever dry up? When?

Krishnayya walked into the water gingerly. There were a few carcasses floating about: rabbits, wildfowl, deer. He could hardly make them out; they were that bloated. They might have drowned in the water or might have died in the wind and rain. They were putrefied and stinking. He thought it was not wise to go on. He turned towards the pathway that was submerged in water and walked back to the village.

When Ganapayya sent word for him, Krishnayya had not been keen on going. In any case, Nagaveni's father had not asked him to go and he felt it was not for him to take a decision. But then, Ganapayya had sent word to his father-in-law too asking for Krishnayya and he had said, 'Krishna, the girl's husband has sent for you. Go and spend these four months with them.' Hoping to escape the situation, Krishnayya had even gone to Sagara on some pretext but as soon as he returned after eight days, his master said, 'Go now'.

And so he had come to Hosamane.

'Nagaveni is Yajamanaru's daughter, ten years younger to me', he mused, 'I've carried her, played with her, and helped her grow.... In those days we always spent time together eating, sleeping, playing. Even as she was growing up, I was fascinated with her. I've noticed her firm breasts under her blouse, her arms filling out, her reddened cheeks, her slender swaying waist. I've wanted to be with her all the time, teasing her, making her cry, making her laugh, comforting her, just being with her. It was a longing, a craze. But her mother would always keep an eye on us, watching over us like an eagle.

'Krishna, Nagu is a big girl now. Don't call her to play with you as you used to do,' she'd say. She must've said something similar to Nagu too.

'Nagu moved from skirts and blouses to saris. Those breasts were covered with a pallu. Yajamanaru got busy with getting his daughter married. The wedding too happened. I had gone right up to the Talaguppa bus stand to see her off. How much she cried when the bus was to leave! I too wept. I couldn't eat the next day. Once when she came home, her mother told her about it and laughed.

'I used to come here once in a way. During my first visit we had climbed right to the cave on Sita Parvatha. But since then I've tried hard to forget Nagaveni. After all, she's my master's daughter. She's married. I'd decided I shouldn't be hankering after her.

'But now, I'm caught in the web once again.

'Nagaveni forgets herself when I'm around. She's not aware that her husband's around. She doesn't need anything else when I'm with her; she's that preoccupied. But who knows where this will lead us? How will Ganapayya view the way we're comfortable with each other? Should I tell her not to be so brash?'

But Krishnayya's selfishness prevented him from asking Nagaveni to be circumspect. He wanted her to behave as she did; to talk excitedly, to laugh helplessly in his presence, to ignore her husband while *he* was around. It gave him a certain pleasure and satisfaction.

This is what he wanted but, at the same time, he did not want to ruin her life. Could the two go hand in hand?

He would have liked to return home. But how? They were hedged in by water that had risen to the level of the tree-tops. And besides, his master had asked him to spend four months with them.

Krishnayya could not sort out his problem.

He came down the hill and started homewards. He took out his girdle, placed it on the platform, and went inside. Nagaveni slipped into the kitchen holding the pallu of her sari to her eyes. She was weeping. Ganapayya strode out looking like thunder.

'Where had you gone?' he asked gruffly.

'I went up to the hill to see if I could return home if the water had gone down,' said Krishnayya in ill-concealed anguish, 'but the pathway is drowned in water ... I'll have to swim to the other bank.'

'Hmm, ... no need to think about that now. Go and see to the cattle. You can go when the water level sinks.'

Ganapayya replaced his frown with a smile but Krishnayya did not respond to it. He could hear Nagaveni sobbing in the kitchen. He dragged his feet towards the cattle shed.

Krishnayya went out again after lunch. Nagaveni came out of the kitchen wiping her hands on her sari. She did not find him on the veranda.

'You know, where's Krishnayya?' she asked as usual. Ganapayya burst into flame like chaff that had been ignited.

'Who's that *bewarsi* to you?' And even before she could say something, he pounced on her, 'If you bring up his name again, I'll hack you down. Take care. I'll break your legs if you walk about in front of him; slit your tongue if you talk to him.'

Nagaveni felt disgusted to hear her husband rave like a low-class man. She was furious too that he could talk to her that way.

'Do what you please', she said calmly, 'Krishnayya's my kinsman.'

Ganapayya was roused even more. He dragged her inside and beat her until he had no strength left.

And then he felt sick; he could not believe he had stooped so low.

'Go and die!' he said and leaned against the bed.

By the time Krishnayya returned, Ganapayya had caught a nap. Nagaveni was still crying. Anger flared up in Ganapayya on seeing Krishnayya but it simmered down and he could talk to him, smile at him. He felt bad that he had created an unnecessary ruckus. As Krishnayya went to the cattle shed, Ganapayya took his knife and went down to the farm.

Krishnayya opened the door of the byre and came towards the house. He saw Ganapayya cross the bridge and go towards the farm and went inside.

'What happened, Nagu?' he asked.

Nagaveni leaned against the kitchen door and wailed afresh. Her unkempt hair, broken bangles, swollen eyes, and her gasping sobs told him everything.

'Did Bava beat you?'

In those days, whenever her mother beat her or her father scolded her, he would ask similar questions. He would comfort her, tickle her, make her laugh. But now?

'I know the reason, Nagu ... I came to help you out only because I couldn't say "no" to your father. Even now I'm ready to go back.'

'It's not your fault at all, Krishnayya. I beg of you. Don't talk of going back. That's his nature. He takes everything seriously.'

'No, Nagu. It isn't his fault at all. *We* shouldn't be so easy-going with each other. Whatever it be, you're *his* wife now. If you talk to me or laugh at whatever I say, he'll naturally feel slighted. Nagu, I haven't come here to ruin your life. I'll stay only if both you and Bava want me to stay. But please don't favour me over him in any way.'

Krishnayya spoke to her like the turbulent river and walked away. Nagaveni stood transfixed as if she had seen her own state of mind.

Krishnayya put on his slippers and went towards the farm.

Ganapayya cut banana leaves, rolled them together in a neat bundle, and headed homewards when he saw Krishnayya walking towards him. He looked grim, purposeful. Ganapayya was filled with fear. Krishnayya could break his bones if he as much as punched him. He was, after all, lanky like a wind-swept tree with not much sap in his body. He thought it would be dangerous to confront Krishnayya. But then again, how could he sit back and watch Nagaveni with this man? How much of a man was *he* if he could not bring his wife to her senses?

Krishnayya met him on the bund.

'Bavayya.'

It sounded like the hiss of a wounded cobra. Krishnayya's eyes were red.

'Bavayya, it isn't fair that you distrust Nagu just because she talks to me the way she does. We've grown up together ... she's like my sister. If you suspect her, it's like you spitting into your drinking water. I came here only to help you out, not for any other reason. If I did have any such heinous desires, it wouldn't be difficult for me to fulfil them. If you don't want me here, tell me so, I'll go back. I'm staying only because I don't know how to explain this to Yajamanaru. This water as deep at the hight of ten men is nothing for me. If you hurt Nagu in any way again, I'll go back without telling you.'

Ganapayya stuck his knife into his girdle and shifted the bundle of banana leaves to the other shoulder. He was struck by the quiet dignity with which Krishnayya had spoken. His words were as impressive as his appearance. The gravity of what Krishnayya had said was enough to shake him up. Faint beads of sweat shone on Ganapayya in the frail monsoon sun. He knew he could not find fault with whatever Krishnayya had said.

'Whatever's happened has happened, Krishnayya. She hasn't been this way before ... I too lost my cool ... Come, let's go back home.'

Both of them crossed the bridge together.

***

'When he asked me what that bewarsi was to me, jumping up and down as if he had stuck his hand in a beehive, it's true I said he was my kinsman.' Nagaveni said to herself, 'I do think he's like an elder brother. But I can't accept that truth all the time; I only said so to quell his suspicion. Krishnayya's truly my companion. As soon as I hear his name, my heart lights up like those different coloured matchsticks we light for Deepavali. It showers sparkles like a hundred flower-pots lit together. It arches like the rainbow from heaven to earth and sets me afire.

'Krishnayya too said something to me before he went out. I'm sure it's come only from the tip of his tongue. It's come so that my husband may not ill-treat me, so that I may not be hurt. But I know what's in his heart. I know he too longs to talk to me, to be near me.'

Nagaveni saw Krishnayya like an aura pervading everything around her. She felt disgust for her husband, repulsion, contempt.

'I've reached a point where I *don't* want to live with my husband. I want Krishnayya. I don't care whether it's dharma or adharma, right or wrong. My spirit longs for Krishnayya and it will not rest until I have him.

'But how ...?

Will my husband let me? Will Krishnayya agree? What will Amma say? What will Appa do? Brothers, sisters, people from our town, from Aralagodu, other friends and relatives? When I think of them, my mind cringes. Instead of being so shameless, why shouldn't I drown myself in the Sharavathi?'

Nagaveni arranged splinters in the fireplace and lit them. She sat with her chin on her hand staring at the tongues of fire that looked like a nude stretching her arms and legs seductively towards the pieces of wood.

She wondered if she was going astray. Ganapayya had taken her hand in marriage with fire as witness. How could she deceive him? She got up from there.

By the time Ganapayya and Krishnayya returned, Nagaveni had washed her face.

Pushya

The rains beleaguered them after an eight-day respite. Dark clouds cast their gloom and the wind howled like one possessed. The cattle that had been wandering about returned to the shed. Krishnayya brought in banana and betel leaves to last for eight days.

As the rain thundered down, he sat on the platform and chewed betel leaves one after the other; this was the only way to fight boredom. Most of the villagers played card games to while away the time. But he had not learnt any because playing cards was taboo in his house. Perhaps he would have learnt a few on the sly if he had not been scared of his master but Krishnayya knew he was dead against such games. Of course, there were other indoor games he would play at home like *pagade* and *channamane*. But with whom could he play them here? And in any case, the kits were with Nagaveni and he did not want to play with her.

Previously, she would have called him.

'Krishnayya, let's play pagade, shall we?'

But that was a long time ago; a long, long time ago. Now he did not have the courage to say, 'Yes, let's' even if she did call him.

The rain fell from the roof like a waterfall. It flowed down the hill and from behind the house and jumped down into a pond in the farm. These sounds mingled with that of the wind and rain to deafen everyone.

Ganapayya was inside. He could be asleep. He had the habit of enjoying a siesta after lunch. Nagaveni too would be sleeping. Krishnayya could have caught a nap but somehow he could not bring himself to sleep during the day. He thought it was not proper to cultivate the habit. Was he the master of a household or a landowner or some lord to eat and sleep? He was only a labourer, after all, working for the food he ate and for the corner where he slept. Why should he develop such excesses?

He stood up looking for something to do. The strands of jute that made up the strings of the girdle in which he stuck his knife were frayed in places. So he got some fresh jute and sat down by the edge of the veranda to roll bits of it on his thigh to twist it into strands. Later he would hold the three strands together and twist them to make the three-ply cord for the waistband.

He heard the jingle of bangles. Nagaveni did not talk to him. He carried on the task on hand, pretending he was not aware of her. When he looked up after some time she was not there. He did not know how long she had stood there at the door.

'Naguuuuuu!' his heart screamed, 'You got married. You entered your husband's house. And I thought you were happy. But what kind of a life is this?' He pressed the strands against his thigh in anguish as he rolled them together. The friction scraped the burning skin, making it red and angry. Nagaveni had stopped talking to him. But she was not talking to her husband either. She was silent as if she had lost her tongue. She did not talk, did not laugh; she only moped and grew thinner day by day.

'Nagu, what's happening?' The question came to the tip of his tongue threatening to ask her but stopped short. 'Who am I to ask such questions? It's better I bite my tongue.'

Krishnayya's mind churned. He longed to talk to Nagaveni but he controlled himself; he could not trust himself. He did not want to ruin her life with her husband. He did not want to come in the way of her happiness, her peace of mind. 'But is she really happy with him? Instead of killing her with good intentions what if I go ahead and give her the kind of bliss I *know* I can give her? Why do I hesitate? What's holding me back?' Krishnayya did not know what was right and what was wrong. He was caught between the two.

He could not sit there and twist the cord any longer. He stopped the task midway, hung it on a nail, and went outside. The thatch was leaking in places. The areca sheath that had been spread on it had blown away and water was dripping on the veranda. But it could be repaired only after the rains. So until then they would have to endure the leaky roof. The farm soaked in the rain, the areca trees swayed with abandon with their palms all askew. The areca fronds bound with sheath swung to and fro with the force of the wind.

'I won't be here to harvest the areca nuts. I shouldn't be here. As soon as the rain stops, as soon as water level in the Sharavathi drops and people start coming this way, I'll go back. Anyway, I have fulfilled the purpose I came for.'

For a moment the rain stalled but only for a moment. Then she charged down the valley with such force that she was like a drape let down from sky to earth.

'Thu!' said Krishnayya, 'this rain is no better than the tears of a woman!'

Nagaveni too was like the rain, weeping for the past eight days; her face, the smouldering clouds, dark and angry; her sighs, the moaning wind from Sita Parvatha.

'And I'm the only one enduring her cloudy, rainy, windy depression. Ganapayya seems hardly aware of what could be happening inside her. He's quite cordial to me. But my anguish is tearing at my guts. Should Nagaveni stay this way? Like low-lying dark clouds? Like raindrops blasted by the wind? Like the wind that whizzes down from the crouching boulders? Should she stay this way?'

As a gust of wind sprayed water on the thatched canopy, Krishnayya stepped back into the veranda.

He wanted to do something to keep himself occupied. His eyes wandered over the tiled roof, the beams, the whitewashed walls, the four pegs shaped like parrots, a creeper strung tight like a clothes-line. Towards this end was the cross pole, the girdle to stick the knife, the knife and Ganapayya's *thundu-panche*. At the other end was Nagaveni's blouse, flapping in the wind and soaking in the rain. What was there that he *could* do?

Ganapayya came outside, red-eyed and sleepy. Retying his panche firmly round his waist, he yawned and stretched.

'Ahaha!' he said, hugging himself to keep away the sudden chill.

'O! Is the younger brother raining instead of the elder one?' he asked no one in particular, referring to the rain easing out.

'And what are *you* doing?' he asked Krishnayya and without pausing for a reply said, 'O, that's good!' looking at the strands of jute he had been twisting to make a new girdle. And then, 'Don't you feel sleepy in the afternoons? Sleeping during the day isn't good, anyway.'

Krishnayya did not say anything. He only smiled at Ganapayya standing there with half-closed eyes, scratching his armpits.

Ganapayya went to the edge of the veranda, rinsed his mouth, washed his face with the rainwater from the roof collected in a cauldron, and wiped it with the strip of cloth on the clothes-line.

'Nagu, get us two tumblers of hot coffee,' he called out as he pulled out a mat and sat down.

Krishnayya sat at a little distance and began to work again on the cord for the girdle.

Ganapayya was talking. It was his usual monsoon-grumble: this year the monsoon was not as good as it used to be.... Won't the rains get scantier as forests were cleared?... Malenadu was becoming barren with trees being cut to make way for railway tracks and highways, telegraph lines and dams and townships for outsiders.... If they continued to hack trees at this rate, of course, the rains will get scarce. And there won't be enough water in the Linganamakki Dam. The Sharavathi Project will be a waste....

'Serves them right,' Ganapayya cursed the government.

'I'm glad they didn't compensate me with land elsewhere and money. I've got a good crop in the fields and the farms,' he rejoiced.

'Krishnayya, have you bought any land for yourself?'

'How could I? Yajamanaru has put by a few acres for me.'

'Really? Get married and start a family, Ayya. How long can you stay in someone else's house?'

'I'm thinking of it. Perhaps next year ...'

Nagaveni came with the coffee. She gave her husband a glass and placed another near Krishnayya and was about to go in when Ganapayya shouted, 'Did you hear that, Nagu?'

She stopped in her tracks and looked at her husband questioningly. He gulped down a sip of coffee and said, 'Krishnayya's getting married next summer. You'll get an Athige!'

Nagaveni stubbed her big toe on the threshold to the kitchen. Krishnayya put down the tumbler he had lifted to his lips.

Krishnayya went outside to check on the cattle. He had let them loose for a while as the rain had let up. That was a mistake; all of them had returned after two hours except Belli. The clouds were gathering force for another onslaught. This rain would pour without ceasing for another eight days. Krishnayya tethered the cows and gave them their feed. Where could Belli have gone?

'Bavayya, Belli hasn't comeback,' he said.

Ganapayya leant against a pillar in the veranda pealing the skin off the raw areca nuts.

'Ayyo, that harlot of a cow has this habit, Maaraaya. It isn't anything new she's started now. She was always like that. She goes to the top of the hill and hangs about the cave. I don't know what she finds there. Maybe her mother's *pinda*,' he said, engrossed in what he was doing.

'I'll go and look for her.'

'Do you know the way? Be careful. There'll be plenty of leeches.'

Krishnayya was frightened of leeches latching on and sucking his blood. So he rubbed oil on his legs and set out.

The path to the top of Sita Parvatha had disappeared under an overgrowth of grass. Krishnayya visualized the previous time when he had gone right to the cave with Ganapayya and Nagaveni and climbed in that direction. Trees, shrubs, and creepers had grown as they pleased because people and cattle hardly went up during the monsoon. And these days, Ganapayya was the only person who cut fresh grass for his cattle. The trees had entwined their branches overhead, making the walk in the gloom eerie. Shrubs shivered as wild creatures scurried about. A rabbit hopped here, a wildfowl flew there, a peacock set up a raucous din from the branches of a tree. Krishnayya wondered how these creatures survived in the rain.

But the forestlands did not continue for long. They were only half way up. Then they gave way to grass that made way for huge boulders. Krishnayya knew he was somewhere near the top from where he could get an overview of the whole area. He walked out of the darkness of the forest, away from the creepers that got entangled with his feet and stood on open ground. Right in front was what looked like the sea, a sea of muddy water. There was water everywhere; wherever he looked, to his right, to his left. And in the distance, beyond the water was the Linganamakki Dam and overflowing from it was the cataract that jumped down and rose up as fine mist to become white clouds in the white sky. Floating in the water were hillocks like tiny islands. These were the remnants of huge hills that the water had swallowed up, leaving only the crests.

'Once the dam is completed, *that* will be the state of this hillock too', thought Krishnayya, reaching the top and surveying the view, 'the water will come right up till here. This hill too will drown completely. And with it, Hosamanehalli, Nagaveni's house, the cave, everything with be covered by the waters of the Sharavathi. The water's flowing away now only because the dam isn't ready yet. Who knows how high it would've risen otherwise?'

'Belli ... Come Belli!'

Krishnayya yelled as he walked about, looking this way and that for the cow. He came towards the boulders. He recognized the one on which he had sat when he came with Nagaveni the first time he visited. Tender memories came flooding of her leaning against a black boulder in a green sari and red blouse....

'Abah, I'm exhausted', she had said, wiping her neck, ears, cheeks, and forehead with the pallu of her sari. She had looked lovely.

Krishnayya remembered how he had gazed at her with love, longing, passion, desire! A fire had flared up in him. But only for a moment; it flickered and went out to see Ganapayya standing in front of them. She was now her husband's property. He felt as if he was pouring the water in his cupped hands back into the flowing river. He had backed out. Even now she was an outsider to him; the cool still water he could never drink.

Krishnayya stood beside the boulder for a while, climbed it, and got down on the other side. And there was the cave. And there was Belli lying in front of its gaping mouth.

'Belliiiii, come ... come ... come, Belli,' he called as he went forward but stepped back quickly. Belli

was not sleeping. She was lying with her head twisted
grotesquely. Blood, red blood lay in huge fresh clots on
the green grass.

'Belli!' he groaned.

The white Belli with three or four black patches
hardly as big as a palm did not flick her ear; she did not
turn to look at him. Instead, he heard a low growl from
inside the cave. Krishnayya had bent towards Belli and
was caressing her when he felt as if someone had splashed
water on him. He straightened, scared. The growl came
again, louder. He backed, climbed the boulder, jumped
down on the other side and hid there.

But the tiger did not come out of the cave. Krishnayya
climbed down the hill as fast as he could, knowing it was
not wise to go forward bare-handed.

Ganapayya slumped when he heard the news. He did
not mind that Belli was dead; he was worried that the tiger
was right behind their house. How could they live there
with the tiger so close to them? How could they walk
about? How much longer would it stay? It had killed Belli
that day. Couldn't it raid the cattle-shed the next day and
the house the day after? Fear gripped Ganapayya again.

The tiger had forewarned them that it was in the
vicinity. But now that Krishnayya said he had seen the
tiger that had killed Belli with his own eyes and heard it
with his own ears, Ganapayya was petrified.

'Did you hear, Nagu? Belli was killed by the tiger,' he said.

She looked at him without any expression.

'I would've been rid of a pest if the tiger had taken you instead,' he ranted, 'what with the water closing in on us and wild animals on the prowl, your long face is all I need!'

The rain that was holding up since the morning started again. Krishnayya stood in the veranda listening to Ganapayya. There was no sound from Nagaveni. The rain started slowly but built up to a steady downpour. And darkness covered the land.

Aslesha

Hosamanehalli was hedged in by muddy water. Creatures that lived in burrows, snake-pits, thickets, caves, and hollows of trees came out of their homes, protesting against the gushing waters and having a free run of the place. With no one in sight and no one within earshot from the world beyond the village and with the three of them becoming one too many, Krishnayya's head screamed for company. There was nothing except the whining wind and the rain weeping like an ill-starred woman, and now ...

He could not laugh his hearty laugh or eat a wholesome meal or sleep to forget his troubles. He could not open out his heart to anyone, could not trust anyone, could not embrace anyone as his own. The householder, Ganapayya, could be feeling the same way. Nagaveni too. Each of them felt shackled to a log and forced to carry it on their heads; Krishnayya winced as if a thorn, embedded in his heel, hurt when least expected. Life had become distasteful.

Ganapayya could not trust his wife. She might have said that Krishnayya was like an elder brother. He too might have accepted her as a younger sister. But Ganapayya suspected they had other feelings for each other. She had called out to Krishnayya to kill the snake. She stared at him as if she desired him, as if she would devour him. True, she had stopped talking to him, laughing with him but then, she had stopped talking to her husband too as if he was wrong in taking her to task.

'What else should I do?' thought Ganapayya. 'Is it possible for me to let her to do as she will; to let her be happy with Krishnayya? If I let her be, Nagaveni might do just that. How can *I* live then? Krishnayya lived in her house. Who knows how things were between them before she was married to me? When she asked me to get Krishnayya here for the monsoon, I didn't realize what was afoot. But now I do. Only, I can't see how this'll end. I thought Nagaveni was naive. I trusted her, loved her, desired her. Can she deceive me this way? Krishnayya calls me Bavayya. Can he stab me in the back?'

The poison worked its way slowly but relentlessly. Ganapayya raged at his wife. He became distant with Krishnayya, almost indifferent.

Nagaveni had arrived at her own decision. All the love and trust she had for the creature called her husband had dwindled the moment he said they should not take refuge from the monsoon in her father's house. And when she had to face the fear of flooding, snake, and tiger, she cut herself from him completely. She shut him out of her heart and mind since Krishnayya was somewhere around, anyway. Now her heart throbbed for Krishnayya alone. She longed to be his.

Krishnayya would have gone home if only the water around Hosamane had subsided, if only there were no wild animals on the prowl around the house. He stayed on mainly for Nagaveni's sake, for whatever pleasure she got out of his presence. He stayed even though he felt his friendship with her might jeopardize her family life.

The water surrounding Hosamanehalli did not sink, the fury of the wind did not abate. The Aslesha rain fell day and night.

***

Krishnayya felt someone shaking him awake and opened his eyes. It was pitch dark with not even a needle-point of light. He felt somehow close to him, someone leaning on him, tender fingers running down his face, neck, shoulders.

'Naaguu!'

'Krishnaaa!' whispered Nagaveni lying on his chest with her face close to his.

'Krishna, why are you killing me this way?' Only when she held him in her tight embrace did Krishnayya begin to realize what was happening.

He trembled imagining what could happen if Ganapayya were to see them. He was appalled by their closeness and even thought of slapping Nagaveni for arousing him. But before he could shove her away, Nagaveni's warm delicate body pressed against his, milking his desire for her. He was vaguely aware of gathering all his thoughts together, putting a basket over them, and setting a grinding stone on it. He drew her into his arms; nothing else mattered.

'Nagu!' he whispered in her ear. She wept like the monsoon, heaving and sighing.

He too sobbed with her and a flood of tears washed over them, drowning them in a shared sorrow. The rain roared and the wind from the Sita Parvatha howled with abandon. The rats in the granary *keech-keeched* as they chased each other. Ganapayya's steady snores came all the way from the inner room to touch their backs.

Krishnayya pushed Nagaveni aside and sat up. He pushed at her slim arm as if to push her away. But when she too sat up and leaned against his chest, he groaned.

'Nagu ... what's happened?' he wept.

'Krishna, I can't live without you. I can't live in this house,' she sobbed helplessly.

'No, Nagu, this is not the way you speak. This is your home. Ganapayya's your husband. You *have to* live here ... Your life can't be ruined because of me. I slipped. True. But this is the first time ... and this is the last ... I'm leaving tomorrow morning ... I'm leaving.'

The thoughts on which he had drawn a basket to cover them when he drew Nagaveni close to him had now pushed it aside and stood staring at him. He felt helpless as if he were looking at the tiger.

'Oh, my God! What's happened?' he cried, all in a dither, 'Did the Sharavathi wash over me? Has she surrounded the house? Has she drowned Sita Parvatha? What should I do now?' And turning to Nagaveni said angrily, 'Nagu, you shouldn't have come to this. You shouldn't have cheated on your husband. You shouldn't have made me do something so wrong. It is done. Now, go away.' He pushed her brusquely.

'Krishna, I've attained moksha. I'm ready to drown in the Sharavathi tomorrow. Today, I've got what I wanted,' Nagaveni said, caressing his arm.

Krishnayya sat stunned. He was only vaguely aware of Nagaveni getting up and going away.

'I've attained bliss.... My desire has been fulfilled.... Who said this?' mused Krishnayya, 'Not Nagaveni at all. She has merely taken the words from my heart and spoken them. I don't know if what we did was right or wrong but those few moments were surely bliss. I too felt an "ah!", didn't I? I too am satiated.'

Krishnayya pulled the blanket over himself and slept. The rain sang a lullaby.

He woke up as dawn was breaking. He could not trust himself to stay on. He knew he would have to be party to whatever else might happen.

'It's best I leave now,' he decided, 'it's not very far from the edge of Sita Parvatha to the bridge that leads to the Aralagodu hill. I can swim across. I just have to steer clear of trees and not get my legs entangled in creepers. Anyway, I've told Nagaveni. Ganapayya will understand. I'll think up a lame excuse to tell Yajamanaru. I can't stay here any longer.'

He got up. He crept softly to the door, opened it, and stepped outside. There was a slight drizzle. He walked on getting drenched; he had forgotten his blanket. Then he remembered Nagaveni. Should he stay back with her? Could he continue to pretend to be her elder brother?

'Thu, disgusting! What happened last night was bad enough. It cannot continue,' he walked on.

Krishnayya walked up the back of Sita Parvatha and down the side that led to Aralagodu. He walked into the water. It was cold. He could see the bridge and was sure he could swim the distance. He took out his shirt and panche, tied them to his head and jumped into the water. There was no point in thinking any further.

The flood had no force in it; the water was quite calm. Throwing his arms forward, stroking the water backwards, he swam a distance and deliberately looked back. Nagaveni was at the water's edge waving at him and asking him to return. Hardening his heart, Krishnayya ignored her and swam on. When he turned again, Nagaveni was not at the spot. Her head was bobbing in the water.

'Naguuuu!' he shouted swimming back as fast as he could.

Ganapayya had got up with a start when he heard Nagaveni scream, 'Krishnayyaaa!' and had run out of the house. Wondering why she had screamed, he came outside. Nagaveni was running on the road to Aralagodu.

He shut the door behind him and followed his wife. He had known things would get out of hand. He now decided he would take a decision, one way or the other. He climbed Sita Parvatha, got down the other side, came to the water farther away from where Nagaveni was and like a passive spectator, watched the scene playing out before him. Krishnayya was swimming away. Nagaveni was standing at the edge, crying hysterically and calling out to him.

Ganapayya hid behind a tree and watched, mesmerized.

Nagaveni shouted for Krishnayya. When he did not heed her pleading cry, Nagaveni jumped into the water.

Ganapayya rushed forward. He saw Krishnayya swimming speedily towards her. For a few minutes, they seemed to struggle, tossing and splashing water upwards. And then there was nothing. The water was still and brooding as it had always been.

Ganapayya did not know whether to cry or to laugh. Should he jump into the water and look for them? Or should he jump into the water and go their way?

He walked back home deep in thought.

As he stepped on to the veranda, he thought he heard a growl. He looked up. It was the tiger.

It sat crouched with its forepaws pressed to the floor and its tail thumping it. It yawned once, licked the air, and looked at Ganapayya hungrily; desiring him.

'Grr,' it growled again. Ganapayya pulled back with great effort the foot he had put forward. The tiger blinked once and stretched. Then, pressing its feet to the floor, it leapt.

Ganapayya opened his mouth to scream.

Water from the Sharavathi continued to girdle the land. The wind from Sita Parvatha continued to blow as it always did during the monsoon. And the Aslesha rain poured as usual without stopping for breath.

The maley-nakshathras that had brought in the monsoon for the year saw it to its end as usual; from *krithika* all the way to *mogge ... ubba ... utthare ... hastha ... chittha*.

***

Glossary

bewarsi	orphan
channamane, pagade	indoor games
chembu	a small round metal vessel
gurudakshine	a gift to the teacher
Hasalaru	the community to which the labourers, Hala and Byra belonged
habba	festival
happala	rice crispies
maunji	a girdle made of munja grass
Mirugi	a colloquial term for Mrigashira
moksha	spiritual release
odyana	waist-belt; girdle

pani-panche	a short strip of cloth men tie around the waist while bathing
panche	a length of cloth men wear around the waist to cover the lower part of the body
parvatha	mountain
pinda	rice offering made during the annual ritual for the dead
raavu	demon
sunna	quicklime
vaidya	doctor who uses herbal medicines to treat his parents

Krithika, Rohini, Mrigashira, Aridhraa, Punarvasu, Pushya, Aslesha, Mogge, Ubba, Utthara, Hastha, and Chittha are stars that influence the different phases of the monsoon.

About the Author and

the Translator

Author

NA. D'SOUZA was born in Shimoga district Karnataka. He worked in Public Works Department, Government of Karnataka for 35 years. His interests are reading, writing, travelling, and participating in activities concerning the environmental. He began writing at the age of 21 and has published forty-five novels, the most famous being *Manjina Kanu*, *Dweepa*, and *Baman*. Many of his short stories and novels have been translated into Telugu, Malayalam, Tamil, Sanskrit, Konkoni, Hindi, and English.

He has been honoured with many awards and received an honorary doctorate for his literary work from Kuvempu University and the Sahitya Akademi Bal Puraskar in 2011. The year 2012 brought the Bala Sahitya Puraskar for *Mulugade Urige Bangavan* from the Sahitya Akademi. Two of his novels *Dweepa* and *Kadina Benki* have been produced as films by well-known directors, Girish Kasaravalli and Suresh Heblikar.

Translator

SUSHEELA PUNITHA was born in Bangalore, Karnataka. She is a former Professor of English, Mount Carmel College, and Centre for Postgraduate Studies, Seshadripuram College, Bangalore. She has written stories for rural children for a UNICEF project called *Children for Change* and has translated Vaidehi's *Vasudeva's Family: Aspruhsyaru* (OUP 2012) and U.R. Ananthamurthy's *Bharathipura* (2011) which was short-listed for both The Hindu Literary Prize and the DSE Prize for South Asian Literature in 2011.